TELEPHONE

A Novel

Percival Everett

Graywolf Press

Many thanks to the Creative Capital Foundation for support during the making of this book.

This publication is made possible, in part, by the voters of Minnesota through a Minnesota State Arts Board Operating Support grant, thanks to a legislative appropriation from the arts and cultural heritage fund. Significant support has also been provided by Target, the McKnight Foundation, the Lannan Foundation, the Amazon Literary Partnership, and other generous contributions from foundations, corporations, and individuals. To these organizations and individuals we offer our heartfelt thanks.

MINNESOTA STATE ARTS BOARD   CLEAN WATER LAND & LEGACY AMENDMENT   TARGET.

Published by Graywolf Press
250 Third Avenue North, Suite 600
Minneapolis, Minnesota 55401

All rights reserved.

www.graywolfpress.org

Published in the United States of America

ISBN 978-1-64445-022-2

2 4 6 8 9 7 5 3 1 A
First Graywolf Printing, 2020

Library of Congress Control Number: 2019948742

Cover design: Kapo Ng

Cover art: Anastasiia New / iStock / Getty Images Plus

For Henry and Miles

I see it all perfectly; there are two possible situations—one can either do this or that. My honest opinion and my friendly advice is this: do it or do not do it—you will regret both.

Søren Kierkegaard

TELEPHONE

Duck Duck Goose

1

People, and by people I mean *them*, never look for truth, they look for satisfaction. There is nothing worse, certain painful and deadly diseases notwithstanding, than an unsatisfactory, piss-poor truth, whereas a satisfactory lie is all too easy to accept, even embrace, get cozy with. Like thoughts that carry with them a dimension of attendant thoughts, so actions have attendant actions, with unpredicted, unprompted intentions and results, good or bad, and things, things themselves, have attendant things in unforeseen perspectives and dimensions. An unsatisfactory truth? Like Banquo's ghost, such thoughts sit in the king's place, literary allusions being all the rage. Such thoughts. It is slavery that inaugurates the path to freedom.

hic et nunc?

I am Zach Wells. Wells is a good name for a geologist-slash-paleobiologist, and so I was one. I knew a lot about fossils and caves, especially the bones of creatures left a long, long time ago. I would tell my daughter that we had to take care of our bones because finally that would be all that was left of us, all that was left to tell our stories. I knew an awful lot about one particular hole called Naught's Cave in the Grand Canyon and the bird life that once lived in it. How arcane is that? Well, I knew more than most people. To make it all clear, I should point out that most people knew more about nearly all other things than I did. All of this was and is of little significance, or perhaps transcendence, except that it clues you in to my profound and yawning dullness. It lets you know that I could spend endless hours with bones, rocks, and sediments, and not only that, but in one very particular cavity in one very particular red wall some forty-four meters above the Colorado River, in a spot that no one can get to except by helicopter or, at one time, a tough-hulled boat. That says something about me, I suppose, if there is much at all to say about me. A friend of mine died in a helicopter crash trying to get to that very particular cave. Asshole that I am, I have returned to the cave again and again and have thought of him only briefly each time. That tells you something, though it's none too flattering.

Before graduate school I was in the Marines. It was a mistake that I never had to regret. I served in no war and maintained no relationship with the corps after I left. I made good friends that I never saw again. I never got a tattoo.

I lived in a town called Altadena in California. It was north of a town called Pasadena. Altadena means "higher dena," as in Pasadena. I do not know what Pasadena means. Apparently no one does. There are many things that no one knows, which is comforting, up to a point. At the time of this writing, I do not know whether I will live much longer, and you don't know what I'm talking about. I was led to this point by a simple note, marks on an odd scrap of paper, words that could have meant nothing, that I could have allowed to mean absolutely nothing. But that's not really possible, is it?

Sicut in spelunca

Aechmorphorus occidentalis. Two fragments found in pack rat middens. Pieces were too small to allow measurement and subspecies identification. The grebe is a common transient and winter resident.

I had a family, a wife and a daughter, Meg and Sarah. I tried to tell my daughter, while she could understand, that women are hunted in this world. I tried to tell her without telling her, without saying it in plain language. I did not want her to be afraid in life. Finally she was not, but that was only because she knew no better. It was a sad, good thing.

Across the long and very old Stanton Street Bridge from El Paso, Texas, is a not-so-little town in Mexico called Ciudad Juárez. Friendship Bridge, Puento Rio Bravo, Puente Ciudad Juárez-Stanton El Paso. Hundreds of women had been hunted there, on the other side of that bridge, pursued, raped, imprisoned, tortured, and killed. They were mostly dark haired and of slender build, as was my beautiful Sarah. Believe it or not, that story is, in a shapeless and vague way, a part of this story.

Some said that two hundred young women had been killed or disappeared in some twenty years. Others said it is closer to seven hundred gone. People are like that about numbers. They will say it is not seven hundred, but only three, two hundred, as if one hundred would not be truly horrible, fifty, twenty-five. No one knew who killed and kidnapped these people. Maybe drug cartels, some said. Maybe roving gangs of sexual predators. Devil worshippers. Perhaps invaders from space. Men. It was men. It was always men. Always men.

The numbers were so very large, obscene, fescennine. Olga Perez. Hundreds of women have no name. Edith Longoria. Hundreds of women have no face. Guadalupe de la Rosa. Names. Name. Maria Najera. It was so uncomplicated, safe, simple to talk about numbers in El Paso, a world away. Nobody misses five hundred people. Nobody misses one hundred people. In Juárez, it was one. One daughter. One friend. One face. One name. Somebody misses one person.

Some people are just no good at being happy. And by some people I mean me. It was not that I was forlorn, not that there is anything wrong with being miserable, or that I wanted to be wretched or blue, but I was not really contented, whatever contented meant, means. That I was not satisfied in life was odd, as I fairly had much of what one would think would be happiness-making. I had a smart, lightsome partner whom, though I was not completely in love with her, I valued and with whom I was satisfied to share the daily, mundane business of life. I appreciated the fact that I should have loved her completely, but being the unhappy wretch I am . . . I had a beautiful child with whom I was completely in love, more every day. Still I had this palpable swath of melancholy that ran through me that I simply could not shake. Our house was warm, comfortable, and, if not big, it was big enough. I had a job studying what I had chosen to study, dry as it was, working with people who were more or less interesting and decent, dry as they were. I was proficient at my work, was recognized for it on occasion, couldn't imagine doing anything else. And yet I would come home now and again, sit in my car in my driveway, and quietly contemplate, coldly measure that most selfish of acts, suicide. The guilt that these suicidal thoughts stirred in me was enough in itself to make me want to kill myself. Don't cry for me, Argentina. The mornings after having these self-centered, idiotic, indolent thoughts were always extremely bright, or at least I was, or tried to be, wanting badly to mask any trace of my despair and self-loathing, a show for the family, for my daughter. I considered that I might have been clinically depressed and rationally understood that there was nothing to be ashamed of were it so, that it was a medical problem, a matter of brain chemistry, but I thought, finally, So what? So what if I was not happy? My happiness was overrated. My daughter was happy. My wife was unworried. But I moved through my life with caution, and caution in love is the most fatal to true happiness.

Teratornis merriami. Three specimens of this giant teratorn were discovered: a partial right humerus and two crania. The crania were obtained in the main room in the 25–50 cm stratum, which is late Pleistocene. After casts were made, the humerus was submitted to the Department of Geosciences at USC for radiocarbon dating. The age was approximately 14,000 BP.

It was a careless, not even reckless, but simply unguarded, move, not in the least like her. She was never unguarded in her play. I studied my daughter's face, observed her brown-eyed focus, recognized it, having seen and marveled at her intensity so many times before. Her gaze was bright, aureate, penetrating, yet this unmindful move seemed somehow important. Easily, clearly a mistake of inattention, one that I would have made over and again, but it was sufficiently uncharacteristic for her that I actually asked if she was certain about making the move. It had been a couple of years since I had put to her such a question and she was puzzled by it, or at least mildly indignant. She watched as I captured her knight with a hardly difficult-to-spot bishop.

"I didn't see that," she said.

"Clearly." I held her captured knight in my palm, not wanting to amplify the event by placing it on the table. "Not like you." She had for a year been a better, much better, chess player than I was. "Anyone can miss something. Take me, for example, I employ such nescience as a tactic."

She didn't look up from the board.

"Are you okay?"

"I think so," she said. She glanced at me, gave the board another steady look, and then resigned, removing her king rather than toppling him, as was her custom. "What the hell is nescience?"

"Tossed it out there just for you."

"Nice word."

"Glad you like it."

"Are you two nearly done?" my wife asked as she passed through the room, her way of saying that someone should start dinner.

"That's my cue," I said.

Sarah followed me into the kitchen. "How could I miss that bishop?" she asked, of herself more than me.

"It happens. We all miss stuff. You probably haven't noticed how handsome I am today. It's because I forgot to shave."

"Yeah, me too."

I opened the refrigerator. "So, what are our options? Is it going to be lamb, or will it be lamb?" I grabbed the paper-wrapped rack.

"Anything but lamb," Sarah said.

"Then lamb it shall be. The due date should be duly noted." I gave the package a sniff, then pushed it toward her. "What do you think?"

She pulled away. "I hate the smell of lamb."

"I think it smells just bad enough to eat. Broccoli and rice to go with?"

"Sure. Might as well live it up. I'll make a salad."

I placed the lamb on the heavy cutting board we'd bought during vacation in New Mexico, then turned to grab a pan for the rice. "The lamb will be good," I said. "Not oversalted and overcooked the way some people make it."

"I won't tell her you said that." Sarah opened the back door and called Basil. The big mutt wagged his away inside. "Who's a good boy?" She loved him up and reached for a treat for him in the cabinet.

"Something little," I said, nodding toward the dog. "Basil-boy is packing on a bit of a tire there."

"Just following his master's example."

"Hey, I resemble that remark," I joked.

Basil wiggled and waited. Sarah asked him to sit for his treat, then handed it over. "A Rathbone for Basil." A family joke that was never quite as funny as it sounded, but it refused to die.

Meg joined us in the kitchen. "Now this is more like it." She sat at the table and watched us. "So, sassy sister Sarah, how was the social studies test? My, that was a lot of *s*'s in one sentence."

"Easy peasy."

"I remember eighth grade," Meg said.

"Oh no," Sarah said.

"I hated eighth grade," Meg continued.

"Why was that?" Sarah peeled a carrot.

"Mrs. Oliphant. We hated Mrs. Oliphant. We called her Madame Elephant, but it wasn't so funny because she was a rail."

"And why did you hate her?" Sarah asked.

"Well, if you're just going to make fun of me . . ."

"No, really, I want to hear it."

"Me too," I said. "Please tell us about Madame Elephant."

"I hate you both. I'll just sit here and enjoy my tea."

"You don't have tea," Sarah said.

"Yeah, about that."

"I'll put on water," I said.

"Thank you."

As happens, just as I was about to say something like *that knife is really sharp*, Sarah nicked her finger. It was easy to forget that she was twelve until moments such as this, when the pain was actually fear. She held her finger in the air in front of her face, staring at it as if in disbelief, her eyes welling.

"Come over here and let's rinse it off. Let's see what we're working with here," Meg said.

I stood back and let her handle it. Meg was good at mothering.

"Oh, it's just a scratch. It's good to bleed a little every now and then, lets the bad stuff out of our bodies."

"It hurts," Sarah said.

"Well yeah, it's going to hurt a bit. A little pain is not such a bad thing. Hurts less already, doesn't it?"

"I guess. Yes."

"I'll get a bandage," I said and turned to open the medicine drawer.

"Just a little pressure and then the band-aid," Meg said.

"It's only a band-aid if it's made by Band-Aid," Sarah said. "Ours are made by Curad, so they're not band-aids, they're bandages."

"Do you and your father rehearse this stuff?"

"Your *bandage*, mademoiselle." I peeled the paper free.

"Merci, monsieur."

"May I?" I asked.

"S'il te plaît."

"Très bien," I said. I wrapped the strip around her finger.

Meg took over preparation of the salad.

Cathartes aura. At least five individuals were recovered, one of those being a juvenile. *Cathartes* appears to become increasingly common at the end of the Pleistocene, perhaps with the extinction of large scavenging birds such as *Gymnogyps* and *Teratornis*.

So often stories begin at their ends. The truth was, I didn't know which end was the beginning or whether the middle was in the true middle or nearer to that end or the other, one being the beginning and the other the end, but, again, which end, or if the ends connected, like a snake eating its tail. So, here I have begun with my daughter, my family, a right place to start, logical and in all ways the center. Though my end is here, was there, my telling unfolds here. Much like the sounds of the birds in the dark outside my tent when I am alone near my cave, my story never hushes. I would lie in my bag and follow their songs one to the next, owls and corncrakes, nighthawks and poorwills.

resulting from autosomal inheritance of mutations in the gene CLN3

I watched my wife perform her nightly yoga routine. My routine was to watch.

"There's something wrong," Meg said.

"What?"

"I have a bad feeling."

"I can't talk to you during downward-facing dog."

"Sorry." She switched smoothly to warrior pose. Slightly better. "Just something in the air."

I nodded. Such a statement would not have meant too much if I had not been feeling the same thing. I didn't tell Meg as much. She was already worried.

"Are you ready for class tomorrow?" Meg asked.

"Did I mention that I hate this class?"

"Why?"

"I'm sick of describing and discussing the formation of rocks with people who are essentially rocks themselves."

"You're a geologist."

"Your point being?"

"Why don't you teach that karst course next semester?"

"Maybe. Are you done trying to turn me on yet?"

"Yes, I'm done. But I'm not prepared for class."

"Well, you read your poems and poem-likes and I'll lie here contemplating the metamorphic rock that is my penis. Perhaps it's hornfels or marble. No, it's novaculite tonight. The rhyming is for you."

"Very nice. I'll be in the den."

"Gneiss, that's what it is. Gneiss is nice. My plagioclase won't last."

"Good night."

"Too late for my slate."

"Good night, Zach."

"Enjoy your iambics."

As I fell asleep, I knew I would dream, and I dreamed first that I knew why I dreamed, why humans dream. We dream, quite simply, so we know we're not dead. Pure blankness, deep, unmoving darkness, would be so terrifying, so paralyzing that we would never wake up.

My dreams were not my entertainment but a lighthouse of sorts. I knew somewhat as I drifted off to sleep that I would dream about my daughter, and so I did. We were, as in life just hours before, playing chess, but the pieces were too large for the squares of the board, and all thirty-two of them were the same color insofar as all of them kept shifting color, red, blue, white, black, all together at the same time, and yet we continued to play. Sarah, her thick hair ever thicker, pulled to the back of her head, hovered her hand over the same knight that in life died so ignobly.

"Don't you see my bishop?" I asked before she touched the horse's mane that was now green, pink, brown.

"What bishop? I don't see a bishop." She stared at me. Her eyes became fixed but not on me, through me.

"Sarah. Sarah. Sarah."

She would not respond. She could not respond.

"Do you see the bishop?" I asked.

But I was not there in her eyes. And in that dream I wondered if she was seeing me, if she was seeing, realizing, at least contemplating the limitations of vision, how we, she and I, could see light waves that were only a fraction of the total spectrum. I thought of my eye's blind spot, that all-too-human blind spot where the optic nerve connects to the retina, the spot the other eye tries to make up for, that hole, a hole where things can disappear or retreat or simply sit. Was I in the holes of both of my daughter's eyes? Her eyes were open, her vision was engaged, but she was not seeing me.

"Sarah. Sarah."

I awoke with a start. I did that so that I would not die.

Falco mexicanos. Four bones of this species indicate at least three individuals: an adult, a male-sized immature, and a female-sized immature. It should be noted that, of the larger falcons, this species, which nests on cliffs, is most frequently encountered in southwestern archaeological sites. Some consider the prairie falcon a statewide resident that was formerly more common.

Meg was asleep in bed beside me. I put my hand on the small of her back. She was warm. It was difficult to know if I was comforted by her presence or her warmth. The truth was that I was not comforted at all. I recalled when my daughter had come into our room every night and climbed into my side of the bed. I never encouraged it, but I never discouraged it either. I knew that it would stop, and it did, abruptly. She was a preteen. It bothered me that it would feel creepy if she had come in now. Yet I wanted her always coming to me; I wanted that child again.

the gene CLN3 is located on the p12.1 region of chromosome 16 and contains at least 15 exons spanning 15 kilobases

I was standing outside my classroom. It being early in the semester, I was about to give for the fiftieth time my lecture on how Eratosthenes calculated Earth's circumference. I was preparing for the glazing over of eyes as math entered the subject.

"Professor Wells?"

I turned to find the young woman who always sat right in front of me in class. She wanted an A, that was clear. I would no doubt give it to her because she sat in the front row and wanted it; it mattered to her. "Miss . . ." I searched for her name.

"Charles. Rachel Charles."

"Miss Charles. Do you have a question?"

"Do you believe Eratosthenes actually used the obelisk at Alexandria, or did he use a scape?"

She was, she thought slyly, letting me know that she had done the reading. I was pleased that she had done the reading, but I was not terribly interested in that fact.

"I just want you to know that I really like the class."

"Thank you, Miss Charles."

"Would you mind calling me Rachel? I don't like my last name."

I studied her stunningly average face. "Why is that? Charles sounds like a good, sturdy name."

"It's my father's name, and he wasn't much of a father. Isn't much of one. So, would you mind?"

"I'm sorry to hear that. Okay, Rachel." I looked at my watch. "Almost time to start, and I have to draw some stuff on the board."

"Okay." She looked down the hallway. "I'm going to grab a quick coffee. Can I bring you one?"

"No, thank you."

She turned to walk away.

"Rachel."

"Yes?"

"Thanks for asking."

I had said her name just so she would know I remembered it.

I felt my shoulders sag as I stepped into the classroom. I knew that the only thing most of the students would remember years after would be the joke "schist happens." Yet none of them would even get "subduction leads to orogeny."

Centrocercus urophasianus. A left coracoid and left scapula from the surface of antechamber 1 are referred to the same individual. Both are in the female size range, as is the surface humerus reported in an earlier excavation. Another, well-preserved right femur was found in a pack rat nest in the upper end of antechamber 1. Its minimum axial length is 68 mm, maximum 73 mm, putting it also in the size range of a female sage grouse.

At home I found a package left by the postman. It was addressed to me, always a thrill. I seldom bought anything online, but I had ordered a tin cloth Filson jacket on eBay and there it was. I set it aside and gave Basil a long greeting, then turned him out into the backyard. I was alone in the house and so fell onto the sofa to enjoy the quiet. I put myself to sleep by recalling my lecture. The last thing I remembered thinking of was my overly excited proclamation that the Greeks knew in 200 BC that Earth was round and about twenty-five thousand miles in circumference. When I woke up five minutes later, my box was still there. I opened it and tried on the jacket. It fit perfectly, was perfectly rugged, was perfectly old fashioned. Meg and Sarah would find it perfectly boring. It was perfect.

I lay back down on the sofa and looked out the big window at the hills. There was not a cloud in the robin's egg–blue afternoon sky. From our house we could see the trails in the foothills of the San Gabriel mountains. I had half a notion to take Basil on a long walk up the hill, but the Santa Ana winds were blowing, and I was sick of the heat. The house was cool and I was comfortable. I would just lie there and get fat like my dog.

My wife and I loved our daughter, and so we were together. Had it not been for Sarah, I doubt we would have continued as a couple. We liked each other well enough and I was a faithful and devoted husband, but I was bored, and I am fairly certain she was as well. But that was okay. I was not bored with my family. I was not bored with my child. I was not unhappy with Meg. I was not unhappy with my job, which incidentally bored me most of the time. I was, to say it again, simply in love with my daughter, with being a father.

Accipiter striatus. One bone, a tibiotarsus in the size range of a female. This species is uncommon in this area now. *Buteo jamaicensis.* Quite common in the area, this species is represented by a complete tarsometatarsus. One burnt and broken buteonine pelvis. A coracoid within the range of at least three buteonine species.

Things developed, as they will, and usually when we speak of such development, "things" means bad things. And so it was.

A bad mark on Sarah's social studies test prompted her to confess that she was not seeing all that well. The whiteboard was a blur. Pages as well. It was an easy enough problem to address and to accept. My wife had worn glasses since early childhood, so it was no surprise to discover that Sarah had her eyes.

The appointment with the eye doctor was on a Wednesday. I didn't teach on Wednesdays, so I took her. The doctor was a pleasant young woman who hummed a lot, more and more as the examination went on. I asked her why she was humming. She didn't answer. She had my daughter stare at a distant farmhouse.

"Is this better or worse?"

"Worse."

"Better or worse?"

"Same."

"Now?"

"Same."

"How about now?"

"Same."

She moved my daughter and took another look at her eyes through the phoroptor. To me the doctor said, "I can't prescribe glasses because I can't figure out what's going on. She seems to be both near and farsighted and neither."

"What are you telling me?"

"Nothing. I can't tell you anything. I think she needs to see an ophthalmologist. I can't find anything wrong with her eyes."

That was, to say the very least, disconcerting. To say the most, it caused me to climb my interior walls like a crazed cricket. I relayed the thin substance of the appointment to my wife and we spent the rest of that night climbing our respective walls, taking turns supplying optimistic nothings.

"What do you think is going on?" she asked again.

"I made an appointment with Dr. Terence. Tomorrow at three. She'll tell us what to do next."

"I've never liked that Dr. Terence. She's always trying to be funny."

"She's a kids' doctor. Anyway, she'll give us the name of an ophthalmologist. If we need one. Might be something simple."

Meg nodded.

Meleagris crassipes. A distal end of a tarsometatarsus was obtained from a pack rat nest. The nest had been burned by vandals, so the bone was somewhat calcined. The fragile specimen was damaged after identification, then restored. The plane of the trochlea and curvature of the distal-most end of the shaft distinguish this species from the common turkey, *M. gallopavo.*

In my dream, a dream that I did not trust from its onset, probably because of the furnishings, I was not myself but instead someone who knew me well and pretended to be me. He, as me, arrived home to sit at the dining room table with a woman who pretended to be my wife and my daughter, who was, in fact, my daughter. My daughter knew that neither of her parents were really her parents, but she didn't let on. She was frightened, quietly so, the worst way to be afraid, more scared than I had ever seen her. Even the fake me was taken by this fear, and wherever the real me was, I was feeling cold deep in the pit of my stomach. My daughter moved her food around on her plate with a spoon, and the fake me found this odd. Her fake mother and fake father talked about things that never happened. Then, in my dream, I complained about my dream, singled myself out as the maker of the dream, then laughed. Laughing, I didn't know if I was me or the pretend me. I awoke with the same feeling.

Some officials in Juárez considered that devil worshippers might be the killers of the women. They sketched a map showing that the locations of past murders outlined a pentagram. People see what they want. With so many sites of murders one could construct a Christmas tree or a poodle's face.

Hilary Gill was an assistant professor. Her area was earthquakes, and unfortunately she had yet to do anything groundshaking. She was extremely young, an attribute that upon her hiring had suggested genius but now after five unproductive years came across as immaturity. She came to see me in the eleventh hour, asking how she might gain tenure and escape dismissal.

"What's in the works?" I asked. "Any papers near done?" I already knew the answer to this question.

"Not really."

We were sitting at a café on campus near the football and soccer practice fields. Flip-flop-clad athletes, men and women, strolled by with their shuffling gaits. Hilary kept looking around uncomfortably.

"Where does your fieldwork stand? What kind of shape is that in?"

"I have a lot of data." Always a bad answer.

I sipped my coffee and watched her as she wouldn't look at me. A couple of years earlier I had instructed her to ignore the advice of colleagues who told her to attend every conference she could. I had suggested that she refuse all committee work. She hadn't followed my advice and here she was, scrambling to make scant data fit into poorly conceived experiments. And, of course, no grants.

"What should I do?"

"I don't know what to tell you, Hilary. Sometimes things get to the point where it's just too late."

"What are you saying?"

"I think I'm saying you should start looking for other jobs."

Hilary didn't show it, but she was weeping. It was then that I had the realization that this was not the first of such conversations she had had. I was not special. She was no doubt seeking out colleague after colleague in search of either a strategy, or at least encouraging, even if misguided, optimism.

"Sometimes it's just too late."

Truth and satisfaction.

While waiting with my daughter to see her pediatrician, my wife and I held hands. I could not remember the last time we held hands.

There was a large aquarium embedded in a wall shared by two

waiting areas, one for sick patients, the other for well. We were on the well side.

Sarah studied a movie magazine. We held hands. My phone sounded. I turned it off and shoved it into the pocket of my newly acquired jacket. In that pocket I found a small slip of paper, the kind of slip that often says something like "Inspected by 53." But this slip of paper said, "Ayuadame."

"What's that?" Meg asked.

"It was in my pocket. It says, 'Ayuadame.'"

"What's that?"

"That's 'help me' in Spanish, right?"

"I don't know."

"I wonder where it came from. I just bought this jacket."

"It's not new," she said.

"No, it was pre-owned, as they say."

The nurse called for us.

Phalarope fulicarius. The proximal end of a right ulna was recovered at the 35–40 cm level. The phalaropes are similar osteologically to the small sandpipers.

A note in a gutter. Does it mean anything? Is there any propositional content without a context? The note says, "the horse is yellow." Found in the city street, does it mean anything? Is there a horse? Is it yellow? Was a child practicing her handwriting? Were the letters typed by a monkey? A sentence by accident? Marks on a page? What if the note read, "the horse is and is not"? It is senseless, but what does it mean?

My daughter loved the infinite monkey theorem. She realized, of course, that the idea did not concern actual monkeys, but she wondered, rather correctly, why that mattered. She laughed and asked, "What if Shakespeare was just hitting keys?"

"Shakespeare didn't have a typewriter," I said.

"What if he was just making marks on paper? And that's how he came up with *Macbeth*?"

"I doubt it. Maybe *Measure for Measure*. I could see that with *Measure for Measure*. Not *Macbeth*."

Dr. Terence was a very young woman. My wife didn't trust her age and lack of experience. I figured she was up on all the latest journals.

"So, what's going on?" she asked.

"You tell her," I said to Sarah.

"I'm not seeing very well."

The doctor tipped back Sarah's head and looked at her eyes while she talked. "Things blurry?"

"The optometrist couldn't find her problem," I said. "Rather, she couldn't solve the problem."

"Okay." She rolled back on her stool. She looked at the chart and noted the vitals, listened to and observed everything much in the way that I might stare at a car's engine.

"Any pain in your eyes? Headaches?"

Sarah shook her head.

Dr. Terence held her hands wide on either side of Sarah's head, well past her ears. "Keep your eyes pointed at my face. Can you see my hands?"

"No."

She brought her hands forward. "How about now?"

"No."

Forward some more, her hands now well in front of Sarah's ears. "There, I can see them."

"Okay."

"What do you think it is?" Meg asked.

"I don't know. I'm going to refer you to Dr. Peterson over at Children's Hospital. He's a pediatric ophthalmologist."

I could see that Meg was unhappy.

"How are you sleeping these nights?" Dr. Terence asked Sarah.

"Same as always."

"Hard to wake up?"

"No."

"What does that tell you?" Meg asked.

"I'm just asking questions," the doctor said.

"I see. So, the ophthalmologist will be able to help?" Meg was leaning forward in her chair, making a show of leaving.

On the way out of the office, Meg said, "That was a waste of time."

I rubbed Sarah's head. "We got the referral. That's what we came for. We'll get this figured out. Right, bug?"

Galinula chloropus. The species is represented by the distal end of a tibiotarsus. This species does not require extensive vegetation for breeding but permanent water and aquatic plants.

That night Sarah went to bed easily and quickly. Perhaps the doctor's appointment on top of a full day of school had worn her out, or maybe it was simply anxiety. If she wasn't anxious before, her mother and I had probably stirred some.

Meg was not tying herself into her usual yoga poses, and I suppose I read this as a gesture.

"The ophthalmologist is squeezing us in three weeks from tomorrow."

"That's the soonest?"

"Apparently."

Meg opened and closed her book.

"What is it?" I asked.

"You," she said, as if she had been waiting for me to ask.

"Me what?"

"Flirting with Dr. Baby."

"What? What are you talking about? I said hardly anything in there."

"Right."

"Are you seventeen all of a sudden?"

"Good night." She turned off her bedside lamp.

"No. What the hell? I think I would know if I was flirting."

"Because you're so familiar with the behavior?" She said this more or less into her pillow.

"Meg."

It was unlike Meg to worry over such things, and so I worried that I had actually been flirtatious. I searched my memory of the brief encounter for something I was missing. I couldn't even remember Dr. Terence looking directly at me during the examination. I tried to be angry with Meg, but I couldn't hold on to it.

"If I was flirting, I'm sorry. I didn't mean to. I didn't realize I was."

"Okay."

Her "okay" was so flat, so distant, so blaming, that it actually did make me angry, and so I said nothing else. Instead I fought the urge to say something mean under my breath, not that I could have come up with anything, and stared through the open window until I believed I was asleep.

I walked Basil up into the hills. I wondered what made any given spot pee worthy. Why did he sniff and sniff at one spot and leave a couple of drops, leave nothing at the next, and then drench another? I asked Basil as much and he offered no answer, at least none I understood. I also recalled as I walked how much I had been softened by my daughter. Since her birth I was a much kinder person. Not that I was ever a mean man, but I was, before her, direct enough, blunt enough, and unfeelingly honest enough to come across as an asshole on more than a few occasions. It surprised me when Meg agreed to marry me but perhaps not as much as my asking her.

On a clear day I would have had a view of downtown far off, but it was not a clear day. I scanned the ground for scat of any animal other than my dog. Occasionally a bear or lion would wander down into the neighborhoods below, hanging out in pools or on porches. It happened frequently enough that the television news caught some on video now and again, but I had never run into anything but coyotes. Coyotes were everywhere. They strolled through downtown Los Angeles at night. Evidence of them was everywhere. I had never even found sign of lions or bears. I was very fond of coyotes, but they weren't lions, bears. I was not afraid of coyotes. There were rattlesnakes up there too, and I was plenty afraid of them, but I didn't want to see one.

"What did you say to Hilary?" Horace Golightly asked me. Horace hated both his first and last names and insisted on being called by his middle name, Igor.

"What are you talking about, Igor?" I asked.

We were sitting in the coffee shop behind the library on campus. We each had coffee, and I was pulling free crumbs from an overly dry muffin.

"When I found her, she was in tears."

"When was this?"

"Couple of days ago."

"I told her she'd screwed the pooch. Not in so many words. I didn't mention a dog. Or screwing, for that matter."

Horace stared at me. "You do have a way with people."

"I told her that it would be in her best interest to start looking for jobs. She's not going to get tenure."

Igor nodded agreement.

"I wasn't going to be one of those colleagues who gives false hope. She needs to be ready for reality. Not that I care all that much. She knew what she had to do, and she didn't do it."

Igor laughed. "You sound like you sounded when we first met."

"Sorry. I'm a little cranky. Home stuff."

"How's work?" he asked.

"Coming along. My grad students are pretty good. The undergraduates are going to kill me."

"You got any hot ones?"

"Come on. They all look like they're thirteen."

"Except the ones that look nineteen." He laughed at himself. "I'm a dirty old paleontologist."

"You'd run for the hills if one of them looked twice at you."

"No doubt. But you, you're a young man."

"I should point out to you that forty-two is still twice their age."

"I hate math."

"Hey, I want you to look at something." I took the slip of paper from my pocket. "I found this in my jacket."

"What is it?"

"I don't know." I handed it to him.

"Help me," he translated it. "What is this?"

"I found it in my jacket pocket."

"So?"

"What do you make of it?"

"Somebody's fucking with you."

"New jacket. Well, used new. eBay."

"Help with what? Homework? The laundry?"

"It's just weird, that's all."

"Weird is the new dean."

I pointed to my half-eaten muffin. "You want any of this?"

He waved it off.

"Do you think I should talk to Hilary again?" I asked.

"No. What could you say?"

"Thought you could help me out."

Igor finished his coffee and nodded toward a young woman walking past.

"What?"

"Don't tell me you didn't see her."

"You know you can count on me to come visit you on every third Sunday," I said. "Now, I'm going to prepare for class."

"I know you. You're going to take a nap in your office."

"As I said."

Fulica americana. Five individuals, represented by twelve bones, were located in pack rat middens. The requirements of this species are very like those of ducks discovered in the cave deposit.

It seemed odd, but right, that Children's Hospital in Los Angeles should be a cheery place. The lobby was lively and colorful. Bright colors, not pastels. A couple of clowns strolled through. Children laughed in the corners with their laughing parents. We checked in at the desk with a smiling young man who already knew our names and which doctor we were there to see. He instructed us to follow the light blue line to the east wing. On our way we passed a giant aquarium filled with angelfish and black ghosts; the angelfish actually had wings. This made me pause, and I stood there staring, a fish staring back at me.

"What is it with doctors and fish?" Sarah asked.

"Fish are supposed to be calming," Meg said. "Fish calm everyone down. They use fish in prisons during riots."

That's not true, I thought, but I said nothing. In what prison were they using fish and how?

The outer waiting area of the ophthalmology department was done up in all red, various shades from pink to burgundy. Our wait for an examination room was, however, brief. The exam room was as one might expect. Posters of eyes and ears covered the walls. A square nurse came in with a clipboard, took Sarah's blood pressure and temperature. She was talking the whole time, but I cannot remember what she said, if I even knew what she was saying. The nurse looked at the thermometer and nodded the nod of an expert at reading such things. "Let's try the other arm," she said about the blood pressure. "The other arm is not the same as that one."

Sarah didn't respond but looked at me as if to ask, What the fuck? And though Sarah would never have said that, not in those words, she actually did. "What the fuck?" she said, ironically.

"Sarah," Meg said. I thought it was a reprimand at first. It wasn't. "Sarah," she said again.

My daughter looked strangely into the air in front of her. Her head fell back ever so slightly.

"Zach?" Meg's voice shot through me.

Sarah was not herself, was not right. I took her hand, felt the small bones under my thumb. I thought it was odd that I was taking time to appreciate her delicate construction. "Bug?"

Sarah's eyes fluttered and rolled back in her head. For some reason I looked up at a poster of the parts of the eye as if for an answer.

The nurse was to the door quickly. "Dr. Peterson!" she called down the hall. "Emergency in three." Then, "Calling Dr. Peterson, calling Dr. P., trouble in room three, Dr. P. I rhymed."

Dr. Peterson was an enormous man, near seven feet tall. He squeezed through the door and gently moved my wife and me out of the way. His giant head hovered over Sarah. "She's seizing," he said. So calmly he said it. But it wasn't his daughter, was it?

And then it was over. Sarah looked at me, disoriented for only a second. I asked her if she was all right. She asked me why I was asking, smiled.

Dr. Peterson stood and bumped his large head on the ceiling. "Whew. An abscene seizure, not obscene, but abscene. But an obscene seizure is something to see, believe you me."

"You rhymed," the square nurse said.

"I believe I did," the doctor said.

I awoke, sweaty and confused. I looked at my watch. I would be only a couple of minutes late for class.

2

There was a bus that transported the gear, but most of the students chose to carpool out to Anza-Borrego, to the Yuha Desert at the south end of the park. It was a two-day field trip that I had made several times. I was in my aged Jeep with Hilary. She had apparently gotten over our last, awkward conversation, but still, there was not a lot of talking during the first part of the long ride. It was near one hundred degrees, and with the soft cover, there was, in fact, no air-conditioning, so we sweated and drank water.

"Think we'll see a lion?" I asked.

"Have you ever seen one out here?"

"A couple of times over the years," I told her. "From a pretty good distance. I think I prefer it that way."

"Just how much chaperoning are we supposed to do?" she asked.

"They're college students. If they want to fuck, they fuck. Who can stop them? It's all cool as long as we don't fuck them. Perish the thought."

"I understand. Though it's really not going to do much to make my job security any worse."

I ignored her comment. "We can't let the underaged ones drink booze. That's the only policing we're required to perform. And all that means is that we don't supply the booze. Might as well accept that they're all going to drink and smoke pot."

"And fuck."

"And fuck."

After some more small talk, Hilary asked if I would write her a letter of recommendation for fellowships.

Turns out I am not a nice man. "Hilary, what kind of letter do you think I can write for you?"

"Never mind," she said.

"No, Hilary, I'm serious. I would like to help you, so tell me what I can write. Do you have anything I can read? Do you even have your raw data in any kind of shape for me to look at?"

"Why are you such an asshole with me?"

At this I smiled. "Good. I'll write you a letter. A good letter."

She tossed me a confused glance.

"If you can tell everybody else to fuck off the way you just told me and do your work, you'll be all right. I'll write you a letter."

"That's all it took?"

"Apparently."

"Thank you."

"What kind of shape is the data in?" I asked, trying to make nice.

"Not very good," she admitted. "I'm really not cut out for this. I'm no scientist. My sister is a great scientist. I'm not."

"I wouldn't say that. You're plenty smart, but as you can see, you don't have to be smart to be successful."

She laughed. "What do you think I should do?"

"I'm not one to offer advice. Mainly because I, unlike you, am not very smart. What do you want to do?"

"Classical piano."

"I didn't know you played."

"I don't."

"A couple of lessons then." I felt more comfortable with Hilary. She had turned some kind of corner, though I don't know what that corner was. She seemed to accept her situation; still quite obviously she was full of fear, but with good nature. I wished I could help, but I knew I wouldn't.

Larus pipixcan. A partial ulna and the distal end of a humerus were recovered from the cave in pack rat middens and on rocks. Some other bones, yet to be identified because of the size of the fragments, were also discovered in similar nonstratigraphic contexts.

I imagined my little Sarah at home. She had not complained about her vision for a few days, and we all seemed to relax a bit. Meg had even begun to talk again about finishing the volume of poems she had been working on for a while. I doubted she would complete the project. For years she had blamed motherhood and marriage for her lost momentum. It was probably true enough. Though I considered myself a present father and capable roommate, it was different for her, as it is different for all mothers. As much as I did, she did more. But at least now she talked about the book the way she once did, and I read this as a good sign, tried to read it as good.

Still, regarding Sarah, or just in general, I had a sense of something looming. I felt myself drifting, sinking, and I didn't want my mood to affect my time with the students, so I started thinking about things like magma formation and subduction boundaries, alluvial fans and headward erosion, canyons and V-shaped valleys.

But the V-shaped valley became a metaphor in my mind for the newly formed watershed that was my daughter's vision. We wondered for months after her birth just what color her eyes would be, dark brown like mine or amber like my wife's. They turned light brown but not amber, so they were her own, and that turned out to be an indication of her personality, always her own person. Perhaps all parents think as we thought about our child's individual and singular attributes, but that made her development no less unique. I always wanted to see through her eyes, to see her world. I imagined, realized, that if I could think like her, have my mind open like hers, so much of the world would be that much more available, magical, mysterious to me. I would be a better scientist, a better person, a better father.

We made a planned stop at a little convenience store in the middle of nowhere, just outside of a nothing called Ocotillo. The flat-roofed, one-story adobe was newly painted, but no amount of cosmetics could cover its age and wear. The sign was not newly painted but spelled out, peeling and weathered, Coyote Stop. We would buy sandwiches and drinks and connect before the last leg of the drive to the campsite. Many of the students had never camped before, so this isolated island of desert commerce served as a bit of a buffer between town and the true middle of nowhere. The ancient couple who owned and operated the gas station had seemed for years as old as the desert itself, and as tough and grizzled as anything that grew or lived in it, but still they carried on. They were both named Pat. Man Pat was a squat man with broad shoulders, clearly at one time quite muscular, and thick glasses. Woman Pat was built similarly, and though she walked with a severe limp, she somehow managed a kind of dancy grace.

"Professor," Woman Pat said as she stepped out into the dusty parking area. She gave me a hug.

Man Pat came out onto the gravel yard.

"Are you still alive?" I asked. "Why hasn't someone buried you?"

"Dying is too expensive."

"That's what I hear." I shook his hand, his grip surprising me, as always. I nodded toward Hilary. "Pats, this is Professor Gill."

"You're too young to be a professor," Woman Pat said. "We're used to these old farts like Zach."

Man Pat shook Hilary's hand in an exaggeratedly flirtatious way, stopping just short of giving her knuckles a kiss. "Professor Gill."

"Hilary, please."

"Did he make you ride in that microwave of his?" Woman Pat asked. "He's not a nice man. Come in and let's find you something cold to drink."

A couple of cars of students rolled in, and the quiet little store was quiet no more. Another car arrived. Rachel Charles got out of that one and waved to me. It made me feel awkward as none of the other students had greeted me at all. Hilary caught my reaction and laughed to tease me.

"Yeah, yeah," I said. I followed her and the Pats into the store. We stood around at the counter and drank soda while the students stocked up on snacks, drinks. I looked at the array of fan belts that hung on the wall behind the register. They were all dusty, and I was fairly certain that most wouldn't fit anything on the road now.

"Excuse me. This is okay, right, prof?" a young man asked, showing me a six-pack of beer.

"You realize that's pretty shitty beer?"

"Yeah, I know, but is it okay if I buy it?"

"How old are you?"

"Twenty-two," he said.

"Then it's okay. But please go easy, and don't share it with the folks who aren't legal, all right?"

"You got it." The lying bastard.

"How long have you been out here?" Hilary asked the Pats.

"Going on sixty years," Woman Pat said.

"You've been married for sixty years?"

"Hell no," the old woman said. "I'm not the marrying kind. This old fool asks me every year."

"But she always says no," Man Pat said. "In fact, she says hell no, just like you just heard. She seems to enjoy saying no to me. I actually don't really have any desire to get married myself, but I ask anyway to make her feel wanted. You can't imagine what it's like to grow so old and unattractive."

"He just talks like that to get me turned on," Woman Pat said.

Rachel Charles came to the counter to pay for a couple of yogurts and some apples and peaches. She looked at me and then at Hilary. To Hilary she said, "I don't know how you can ride in that Jeep without air-conditioning."

"It's not so bad," Hilary said, then shook her head. "Actually, it's hot as hell. It really is uncomfortable."

"We could trade," Rachel said. "Trade vehicles. I'm in the Audi with Danica. It just feels so comfortable I don't think I'm in the wilderness."

"Well, I don't know." Hilary looked at me.

I hoped she could see that I was begging her to turn down the offer. I didn't want to make an issue of it by inserting myself into the discussion.

"Danica is in your section anyway, Professor Gill, and I know she'd like to get to know you better," Rachel said. She was sounding pushy, if not desperate.

Hilary caught my eye for a second and then said, "I need to stay in the Jeep. Professor Wells and I have to discuss our lectures."

"Oh, okay." Rachel left us.

"Thank you," I said.

"Someone has an admirer."

"You think?"

"So, how do you handle something like that?"

I looked out the window at Rachel leaning against the Audi, chatting with her classmates. I was afraid to imagine what she might be saying.

"Does it worry you?"

"It happens. You just ignore it and it goes away. I can't imagine what's going on in that brain of hers. I realize that I'm a beautiful specimen of a man with a dazzling intellect, but I'm twice her age."

"Exactly," Hilary said.

"Now, see, I just don't get that. Are you talking about daddy issues?"

"Some call it that."

"In six years my daughter will be that student. Six years. What do you think I should do?" I asked.

"You could kiss her and scare the hell out of her."

"You're joking, right? Yeah, you're fucking with me. Can you imagine what would happen if I let her kiss me? What would you do?"

Hilary looked at the tray of candy bars on the counter, handed one to Man Pat. "I'll take this," she said. Then to me, "I'd do what you're doing, pretend it's not happening. But sooner or later you're going to have to say something."

"Well, let's get these people moving." I thanked the Pats.

Everyone paid up and we were on the road again, this time as a convoy, moving slowly behind the bus on the gravel road. Thirty minutes later we were standing in the harsh midafternoon sun erecting the awnings for shade.

Hilary called for everyone to "get hydrated" before the afternoon's short hike under the sun and before her lecture. As I watched her, I appreciated her youth and thought she was, in fact, pretty good with the students, better with them than I was in many respects. So she wasn't going to shake up the world with her research and scholarship. I'd published many articles and hadn't shaken much of anything. Rachel was near my Jeep talking to one of the football players in the class, leaning close to him in a flirtatious way. For a moment I felt a bit of relief, and then I caught her stealing glances at me, and when she caught my eye she leaned closer to the kid. The athlete was taken in. It was quite sad.

I shook the trouble out of my head and called for everyone to get ready for the hike. "It's not a long walk, but bring your water. Professor Gill will lead the way and I will be at the rear. Let's move quickly so that we can be back well before dark. Okay, Professor Gill, take us out of here."

We walked beneath the old washed-out highway bridge and along the ragged ridge that led south. The sun was intense as the sun was always intense out there, and I watched the students closely from behind. It was the athletic men who seemed to complain most. At first I thought it was ironic, until I understood how much attention their complaining attracted from the women in the group.

We stopped and I lectured. "These are the oldest rock bodies found in the area. These metasediments date back to the early Paleozoic era. Who can tell me what a metasediment is?"

Of course it was Rachel Charles who offered the simple answer to my simple question. She had read her homework, of course. She smiled at me, and I told her she was correct while looking away.

"This is an alluvial fan deposit that is made up of red sandstone and boulder conglomerate from the middle Miocene, more than twelve million years old. There are several layers, but all I want you to do right now is find some examples of the youngest rocks. Remember your lab work and find sandstone and marine turbidite. And also see if you can locate oyster shells, mollusk, and coral."

"This will go faster if you work in groups," Hilary said.

The students managed to work out teams of three, and somehow Rachel managed to be the odd person out. "I don't have a group," she said to me.

Hilary stepped in. "I'll work with you. What's your name?"

"Rachel Charles." This was offered flatly. Rachel's sullen face only served to underscore her youth, and for a flash of a second I saw my Sarah and her approach felt even worse.

The hike and lectures went their tedious and boring ways. The students, despite their complaints, didn't seem to suffer greatly in the heat and they paid relatively close attention, with the normal jockeying to stand next to whatever creature attracted them. Again, Hilary was completely at ease, a natural with them. I wanted to be able to tell her with some confidence that the research would fall into place, but I honestly did not believe that to be in any way true. She was also admirably comfortable maintaining her boundaries with the male students who found her attractive, desirable. She never showed any panic, as I am certain I did. The young men merely wandered off, confused but unhurt, yet clear on their standing.

Back at the campsite we put up tents, laid out sleeping bags, and ate food that didn't need to be cooked. The sun fell and then the temperature. The students split up into little groups, laughed, drank beer and other things. It was nearly cute how they attempted to hide the booze from me. They paused at the occasional howl of a coyote.

"Professor Wells," a male voice called to me.

"Yo!"

"Is it true there are lions out here?"

"Yes, there are cougars out here," I said. "But you'll never see one. You might see some coyotes and even a tortoise, but the lions knew we were here before we did." I looked around at them. "If you do wander off, don't go far. It's easy to get disoriented out in the desert because every direction looks the same. We don't need to spend any of our time searching for a lost one of you. If you're by yourself out there, you might just see a lion. Worse, he might see you."

Later, when things were finally quiet, after Hilary had retired to her tent, I decided to take a walk around, to be alone, to enjoy the desert, and to be sure no one had wandered off and become lost. The full moon made it easy to see, placing doughnuts of shadows around the greasewoods. The light also made it easy to imagine that one knew where one was. The sky was black, deep, infinite, the very thing that scared the Greeks.

If I had heard their breathing, I would not have walked closer, but I had not heard them, and so I found myself observing, unobserved myself, two students fucking. I stopped dead, and as I turned to fade back into the darkness, I saw that the young woman was Rachel, and just as I recognized her, she saw me. She was sitting on the man but made no move to get up, offered no reaction that might have alerted her partner. I froze, watched as she watched me, watched as she pushed harder down onto the man. She would not look away from me. Actually, she stared right at me; turns out there is a qualitative difference. We must have shared, or perhaps split, no more than a couple of seconds there before I escaped, but I caught myself with the strangest feeling of, first, jealousy, then protectiveness as thoughts of my Sarah came to me. Neither feeling was appropriate, nor did either make any real sense to me, at least no sense that I wanted. I returned to the camp and crawled into my sleeping bag, set off some yards from the students' cluster of tents. I drifted off to sleep looking up at Gemini, Orion, and imagined I could just make out the faint Monoceros. It struck me, as it always struck me, how little I knew about the stars. No matter how much I read, I never knew more.

I found sleep or it found me. And in my sleep I dreamed, or perhaps I didn't sleep at all and merely entertained anxious thoughts. My dreams or ruminations were disturbing, and I wondered during them whether my imaginings then would have been more disquieting, alterative, as thoughts or dreams. I dreamed or imagined Rachel Charles riding the man in the desert. She was naked, though she hadn't been when I saw her, and there was light now that allowed me to clearly see her breast, the muscles of her flat stomach. In the dream, or whatever it was, I found her attractive, and I had an erection that I found embarrassing because I should not have had one, in fact had not had one at the scene. I was embarrassed in my bag to merely find the young woman attractive, and also because I thought my condition, if you will, might be visible from outside my sleeping bag. In my dream, or my thinking, I decided it didn't matter what I was experiencing. Finally, it was sleep.

I awoke to another kind of excitement, hushed screams, if such a thing is possible. I pulled on my boots and walked toward the commotion. "What is it?" I asked.

"A snake," a man said.

Sure enough there was a good-sized rattlesnake coiled on the pink sleeping bag of a young woman I knew to be a song girl with the marching band. The snake lay still between her raised and trembling knees. I was not so alarmed by the snake but by the thought that she might try to squirm out of her bag. Of course, the snake was not on top of me. The woman was beside herself, though appropriately frozen. What was alarming now was the sight of one of the muscly and overly confident athletes reaching for the head of the creature. Before I could tell him to back away, he had grabbed the snake's head just as he had imagined it was done on nature television. Unfortunately, he pressed his thumb onto the top of the animal's head, and the snake slowly coiled around his arm. The look on the kid's face was almost comical and yet it was not. I had had some experience with rattlesnakes but was hardly an expert, but even I could see he was in trouble.

"First of all, don't let go of its head," I said. "What's your name?"

"Calvin."

"Okay, Calvin. What sport do you play?"

"Baseball."

"Good. Keep a firm grip for me. Mind if I tell you that was a stupid thing to do, grabbing this thing?"

"I realize that now."

I grabbed the snake's tail, the skin rough against my fingers, and unwound it from his arm. I could tell it was still cold, cold enough not to rattle, and that was a good thing. "Hilary, would you grab a tent bag or something?" I could feel the snake coming around, aided by the heat in the air and our hands. Hilary returned with a sack. The snake was waking now, writhing.

"What now?" Calvin asked.

"Shove his head in the bag, but don't let go." Calvin did. "All right, I'm going to grab its head from the outside. Don't let go until I tell you." Calvin nodded and I grabbed his wrist from outside the bag and worked my way to his fingers, then grasped the rattler on either side of its head. "You can let go," I said.

"Thank God," Calvin said.

I pushed the rest of the snake into the bag and cinched it closed.

The students applauded, rather weakly. I hated the attention and moved off with the snake. I stopped and turned back to them. "What Calvin did was reckless and stupid. No offense, Calvin. If you see a snake, just remain calm and call me or Professor Gill." I turned and walked away.

Hilary caught up to me. "I don't want them calling me when they find snakes," she said, almost laughing.

"Hell, I don't want them calling me either. At least you'll be calm and not do something crazy like Calvin back there."

"What are you going to do with the snake?" Rachel asked. She had trotted over after Hilary.

"I'm going to let him go."

"May I come?"

"No," I said without further explanation or discussion. I didn't even look at her eyes. I was afraid she might follow anyway, but she didn't. I walked farther perhaps than I needed and rather unceremoniously set the animal free in a wash. It didn't move away but did raise its head, smelled the air, ignored me. I did not take this personally. I looked at the anhydrous hills and was overcome by sudden formless, unshaped worry. I needed the snake to move before I left that spot. I grabbed an ocotillo branch and touched the rattler. It slithered off without rattling, much in the way I had walked away from Rachel.

Branta canadensis. The five bones from pack rat nests are from at least three different individuals. One femur and an ulna might be *Branta canadensis parvipes*, known to winter in the state.

Late that afternoon, after the hikes and lectures and the oppressive heat, many of the students decided to make the longish drive back to Los Angeles. A few wanted to camp one more night, it being a long weekend, something about Columbus. If any were staying, I was staying. Hilary chose to remain as well. The smaller group did not sort themselves into clutches but remained together sitting around a fire. Of course Rachel remained. I didn't know if her sexual partner from the previous night was there or not, as I never saw his face. Regardless, she unfortunately seemed unattached to anyone there and kept a conspicuous eye on me through the flames. We did the cliché thing of roasting marshmallows and hot dogs and actually listened to one another. Hilary got them talking by asking if anyone had ever been lost. A couple had stories of being lost as children.

"What about you, Professor Wells?" from Rachel.

"I've been lost more times than I can count," I said. "Being lost is a good thing. Generally, a good thing. It's a good thing if you get found. I was lost not too far from here about twenty years ago. I was part of a search party looking for a lost girl. She was ten, if my memory is correct, and had gotten separated from her parents. I wandered into what I thought was a box canyon that turned out not to be a box canyon, and I got turned around. At first I couldn't believe I was lost, but I caught on pretty quickly. No one had cell phones back then, and they wouldn't have worked out here anyway."

"What did you do?" This from a woman who looked alarmingly like Rachel Charles.

"I found the highest ground I could and looked around. I was certain I would see other members of the search team, but there was no one. I considered panicking for a couple of minutes, realizing that no one would think to look for one of the searchers. I had some water and I found myself measuring it, thinking about rationing. I stayed there on that ridge and night came. I thought I was going to freeze to death, it was so cold."

"Then?" a young man asked.

"I shined my flashlight out into the darkness, but nobody saw me. Morning came and I decided to walk back in the general direction from which I had come. I walked for miles. The sun beat down on me. I could feel my tongue swelling slightly. I was dragging my feet. I tried to get water out of a prickly pear, but I didn't know what I was doing."

"What happened?" Rachel asked.

"Oh, they never found me. I died out here."

They laughed not because I was funny but because I had caught them. We sat around a little longer. A girl with a guitar sang a song that I didn't know and didn't much like, but it was sweet, old fashioned, her doing that.

It was suddenly late, and as I looked at their faces, it dawned on me that they were afraid of turning in because of the snake incident. "I think I'm going to turn in," I told them. And I left them there.

I grabbed my canteen and wandered far off so I could brush my teeth and pee in peace, then returned to my bag. I was tired and my legs ached, though I'd done very little. This made me feel old. I removed my shirt, boots, and belt and slipped in. I was nearly asleep when the crunch of footfalls came close. I looked up to see Rachel.

"What do you want, Rachel?"

"I'm afraid of snakes," she said.

"Don't worry about snakes. The snakes don't want you. You're too skinny to keep them warm."

"I can't get them out of my head."

I sighed, studied her ever so briefly, and grew slightly irritated. "You do understand that I'm your professor, your married-with-child professor?"

"It's the snakes."

I wanted to say that she should have left for Los Angeles with the others, but I didn't. It didn't make sense to comment on something that was done and over. "It's hardly likely that that will happen again, a snake showing up in camp," I said. "Get in your tent and zip it up. If by some incredible magic a snake shows up, it can't get inside your zipped-up tent."

"Really?"

"They don't have hands, Rachel."

She laughed.

"Good night, Rachel."

"I'm scared. Can't I just sit here and we talk for a while?" Before I could scream for help, she was seated on the ground.

I sat up in my bag. "There's not much for us to talk about."

She said nothing but looked at the quiet campsite.

"What are we supposed to talk about?" I asked. "What do you want to talk about?"

"Anything."

"Where are you from, Rachel?"

"The Seattle area."

I nodded. "Siblings."

"Nope. My mother had a miscarriage before I came along. She says she was lucky to have me."

"No doubt."

"What about you? Where did you grow up?"

"Durham, North Carolina."

"Do you have any brothers or sisters?" she asked.

"No."

She used her finger to draw in the sand in front of her, something she couldn't see in the dark. She raked her dark hair behind her ear and offered a nervous smile. I hoped she could sense how uncomfortable I was. I looked back at the quiet campsite to see if anyone was observing us. No one was.

"What's your major?" I asked.

"Biology. But I'm thinking of changing to geology."

"Why is that?"

"You," she said, happily. "You seem to love your subject so much."

I had never heard such bullshit in my life. I opened my mouth and said, "I have never heard such bullshit in my life."

Her face went blank. Blanker.

"Really, Miss Charles, do you think I will date you? Kiss you? Sleep with you? You don't know how I feel about anything. I have taught you a few terms about sediment and rocks and watched you have sex for a nanosecond. I didn't even watch long enough to have any interest."

To her credit she did not cry in front of me, or perhaps at all. She got up and marched away without a glance back at me.

I felt like shit. I was a shit.

I didn't sleep that night. And not because of snakes. Perhaps in some perverse way it was because of snakes. I got out of my bag and walked through the desert. My footfalls were heavier than normal, and so my own noise bothered me.

3

I returned to find my home empty. I stepped out into the backyard and saw that some clouds had started to gather in the western sky. The temperature was dropping, and I wondered if we might be lucky and get some rain. Like most Angelenos I resisted believing any promise of precipitation, even, maybe especially, if made by the sky itself. Basil was happy to have me home. He considered the manner in which I ignored him a kind of attention. He and I were not so different.

That night, as I prepared to shower off the last of the desert dust, I told Meg about Rachel Charles. I mentioned it only because it bothered me so much, made me sweat like I was about to be electrocuted or something equally unsure to work. I wondered why it

unsettled me so and even considered momentarily whether bringing it up was a wise thing to do. It was not. I thought I was being
open, honest, clean handed, but apparently I was being egotisti-
cal, insensitive, throwing a young girl into the face of my middle-
aged wife.

"You must have been very flattered," Meg said in way that had
nothing to do with my being flattered.

"Well, I wasn't. What's eating you?"

"You loved it."

"As a matter of fact, I didn't. I hated it. I was embarrassed by it.
I'll ask again, what's the matter with you?"

"Why are you telling me about her?"

I paused to look at her, still in my skivvies. "I'm telling you because that's what we do, our being married and all."

"I don't want to hear about it," she said. She grabbed a book from
her nightstand. "I have no interest."

"Duly noted. I won't mention it again."

"Don't patronize me."

"I wasn't patroni—I didn't mean—All right, I won't do it." My
head was swimming. "I'm going to go get clean now. Okay?"

When I came out of the shower, I said, "I absolutely was not flattered by that young woman's attention. I am truly sorry I told you,
but I was simply sharing. I'll know better from now on."

Meg said nothing as I pulled on my pajamas and left the room.

That night, instead of sleeping, instead of restoring my body, because that was what I was told and believed sleep was for, instead
of dreaming and so, subconsciously or unconsciously (I could
never keep those straight), sorting out whatever waking-life problems that were eating away at me or that I was afraid to face, I sat
up and stared at the small strip of paper I had found in my jacket.
"Help me," it said in Spanish. Perhaps it was a joke or merely a message from one tailor to another, a plea for assistance getting a seam
straight, making sleeves the same length. Regardless, it carried no

weight in my real world. There was nothing for me to do, say, or consider. As that had never stopped me before, my never having been a depository of good or even common sense, I opened my computer, logged onto eBay, and looked to order something else from the vendor who had sold me the jacket. I found and bought a shirt with two flapped breast pockets.

Anas platyrhynchos. There are thiry-seven occurrences of the species from the cave. There have certainly been changes in the distribution of this hen-feathered population since the Pleistocene. The mallard is a common transient and winter resident where there is open water.

Sarah claimed that her vision had not deteriorated further, but she was not seeing as she had. Dr. Peterson was not what I had dreamed. He was in every way average, height, weight, humor, and strangely all of this ordinariness served to promote confidence in his ability as a doctor. He was at ease with Sarah, patient while listening to us describe the situation, and remarkably calm as my daughter slowly and quietly began to have the very seizure I had dreamed she'd have.

"Sarah, how is your vision today?" Peterson asked. "Sarah?" He leaned forward to look at her eyes.

"Okay," she said.

Peterson looked at her eyes. He paused, adjusted his light, and studied the left one again. He made a note. "Sarah, would you look to your left, please, away from the light? Sarah? Sarah?"

Sarah looked disoriented. She smacked her lips in a way that was unfamiliar. She had never done that before. Meg looked at me. I had never been so alarmed by any sound in my life.

"What's going on?" Meg asked.

"Sarah?" Peterson was quietly alarmed now.

Meg and I, not so quietly. "What's wrong with her?" I asked.

After a minute, she was staring back at us. "What is it?" she asked.

"Are you all right?" Meg asked.

"Sarah, do you recall me turning to look at your eyes?"

Sarah didn't answer, but it was clear that she was confused and quickly becoming scared.

Peterson measured her pulse and wrapped the blood pressure cuff around her arm, inflated it while he studied her face. "How are you feeling?" he asked.

"Mom?"

"Just relax, baby," Meg said.

Peterson released the cuff. "Everything sounds good."

"What just happened?" I asked.

"Could have been nothing," the doctor said. He got up, opened the door, and called in a nurse. "Lacy, would you take Sarah down and get her height and weight for the chart?"

Sarah looked at Meg, then to me. I nodded. "Go on."

Once the door was closed, Peterson sighed. "Could be nothing, like I said. But your daughter might have just had a seizure, what we call a complex partial seizure."

"What does that mean?" I asked. "What does it indicate?"

"Maybe nothing," he said.

"People don't have seizures for no reason," Meg said.

He took a pad from the pocket of his white jacket and started to write. "I don't like to guess about anything. I think you need to have a neurologist see her. Dr. Gurewich is in this building and she's very good."

"What are you thinking?" Meg asked.

"Dr. Gurewich is excellent."

The drive home was as awkward as any I remembered. Fear had not settled in but was looming. Sarah did not take her customary seat, right-hand rear, but instead buckled herself into the middle. Her confusion was manifesting as anger, a generalized, unfocused, silent rage. I daresay I was feeling some rage as well, as unfocused as hers, and I was doubtless no less confused.

Finally, "What did the doctor say about me?"

"We have to go to a different doctor," Meg said.

"He didn't even look at my eyes."

"I know, honey."

Olor columbianus. Two mandibles recovered from a pack rat nest. The species is a winter resident in Arizona. It will rest in deep water; however, it uses its long neck to feed from the bottom of shallower water.

A seizure. Sulking, if one could call it that, in the backseat, she seemed so normal, so much herself. I immediately thought that the seizure must have been brought on by a brain tumor. I reminded myself that I was no physician. I reminded myself as well that Peterson had not stated certainly that my daughter had had a seizure. I glanced at Meg, who stared straight ahead through the windshield.

"It's good that we can see Gurewich tomorrow morning," I said.

Meg did not reply but kept her gaze forward.

The worst feeling in the world is knowing your child is afraid, not startled or apprehensive as when about to take a test or ride a roller coaster but paralyzed by that icy cold in the pit of her stomach, confused because she suddenly believes her parents cannot make it all okay. When Sarah broke her tibia playing volleyball, I was of course concerned and hated that she was in pain, but that was manageable. Now, there might have been nothing wrong at all and certainly I was afraid, but the look of fear in Sarah's eyes sent that same ice lance through my center, lodged it in my spine, and stayed there, unmelting, unmoving. My daughter was my reason for waking each day, and I wanted to kill myself for having in some fashion already resigned myself to losing some part of her. Selfishly, I saw my world as illusionary, fragile, existing only because others allowed it to exist. I realized that I was ever awaiting such a moment of loss, that I was, in fact, daily resigned to death but had never resigned to life. I bit my tongue hard enough to snap out of it.

But not hard enough to injure myself.

As always, though I could get caught up in a swirling current of anxiety, I was a lightweight compared to Meg. She was aerial; she could latch on to an optimistic balloon, ride it high, and then let go, spiral into despair at the prescribed acceleration of thirty-two feet per second. It is very difficult to catch someone falling from a dizzying height. It was good for neither fallen nor catcher and sadly was historically the reason for our disconnectedness. I understood at once and disappointedly that my spiraling was an unconscious effort to ignore the fact that something was wrong with my daughter.

As Sarah's appointment was in the afternoon, it seemed advisable to send her off to school, an attempt to give her the impression that all was normal in our eyes. I too was off to school to face my auditorium full of rock-bored underclass folks. Still, breakfast was a quiet affair, which saw us seated at the table together, a rare configuration, as I usually ate standing between the sink and refrigerator while Sarah sat at the table while Meg consumed nothing at all, spending her morning gathering her students' work. This day was a nonteaching day for Meg, and I observed her unsettledness. I felt relieved that I had someplace to be and something to do, even if it was describing the geologic features of the relatively small alluviated lowland that was the Los Angeles basin.

Anas discors. Four bones of this species were found, identifications based on the diagnostic tympanum. The blue-winged teal is the rarest of the teals in the region.

I was standing in the doorway to the lecture hall when Rachel Charles walked past me. She was quite obviously still unhappy with my having blocked her attention that night in the desert, but it seemed she was no less interested in me. This I gleaned from her protracted sidelong glance and her clothes, which were somewhat more revealing than usual. She sat in her customary first-row seat and conspicuously crossed her exposed legs. That I noticed at all made me feel bad. With her eyes down the entire period, she appeared to be taking notes. I found the absence of her gaze slightly more disconcerting than the adoring, fixed, and hungry stare that I had grown so used to apprehending. The most annoying effect of her newly found motif was that it served to arouse me somewhat, an arousal that I immediately recognized as another attempt on my part to ignore what was happening at home, but that made it no less shameful or opprobrious. My lecture ended with a description of the Playa del Rey, Inglewood, and West Newport oil fields and the threat that I would continue the same lecture at our next meeting. The students collected their things and made haste out of the room as they always did, and as she always did, Rachel was quite slow about packing up until she was, in fact, the last one leaving. She still hadn't looked at me as she headed for the door.

"Rachel," I said.

"Yes, Professor Wells."

"Are you all right?"

"Why wouldn't I be?"

"I hope I didn't hurt your feelings the other night."

"Well, maybe. But you were right. Why would someone like you be interested in someone like me?" And then she walked out.

I had to admit that it was an unsatisfying exchange, and yet I was happy it was so abruptly concluded. What would I have said if she had lingered? Lord knows. It could not have been good, that was all I knew.

Hilary Gill was waiting at my office door. I suppose that we had bonded somewhat on the field trip, but her presence was still unexpected. Without much of a hello she launched into her request for a favor. It started with, "I was wondering . . ."

"What do you need, Hilary?"

"Will you look at my data?"

"I've got a lot going on at home right now."

"Just a glance. No rush. Well, a bit of a rush."

"No promises."

She put a USB drive into my hand. "Thank you, so much."

"Okay."

She started to walk away.

"Hilary." When she turned back to me, "I can't make any promises."

"I know."

We performed well enough in the scene that preceded the afternoon appointment with the neurologist. We prepared as if headed for a routine visit to the dentist, Meg even reminding Sarah to brush her teeth, a request that made no sense and somehow all the sense in the world. In the car we listened to "Sarah's" music, always worse in theory than in practice. At least for me. The sappy pop seemed to irritate the poet in Meg, but I had to admit I sort of liked it. While a girl sang a cheery, up-tempo ditty about happily casting off the devastating hurt of lost teenage love, I reached over and squeezed Meg's hand. She rubbed her thumb against my knuckle. And thus was the only expression of panic during our ride. I continued to be an agreeable audience to my daughter's tunes and recalled first bringing her home after her birth. I thought as we were leaving the hospital, Are they really just going to let us stroll out of here with this person? But they did. No one warned us about the sounds a baby was likely to make in the night or how they might seem to stare ghostly at you in the darkness. Sarah gurgled crazily while sleeping, causing us to think she was choking to death. I would leap up and rush to her side only to have her noise subside into the most peaceful breathing. When I didn't tear myself away from the sheets, her gagging would become eerily absent, and so I would spring out to be sure that she was still breathing. Most of my parental sleep deprivation was a consequence of my anxiety over keeping this creature alive. And so, here I was again. When I looked in the mirror at Sarah in the backseat, I found her staring at me, wanting me to make it all okay.

Aythya valisineria. Eleven individuals of this species are represented in the cave. The humerus of this species is distinguished from *Aythya americana* by the shape of the proximal end. In modern times, the canvasback is an uncommon migrant. It winters on open water.

I suppose anytime someone is seeing a pediatric neurologist, it is given that there is an abundance of anxiety, and so our wait in the outer area was notably brief. The doctor joined us in the examination room almost immediately.

Dr. Gurewich was a broad-shouldered woman with a noticeable accent, I thought Eastern European. She talked to the three of us first, questions about Sarah's schoolwork, her vision, her diet. She then called for a nurse to take Sarah and get her weight.

She turned to Meg and me and asked about the alleged seizure we might have witnessed. We told her what we knew, what we thought we saw. She asked if we'd noticed any new behaviors, tics, sounds, sleeping problems.

"Nothing," Meg said.

"She didn't see my bishop," I said.

"What?" from Meg.

"We were playing chess. She's a very good, careful player. She didn't see an obvious danger."

"What's that have to do with anything?" Meg asked me.

"No," Dr. Gurewich said. "It's a bit of information. It might mean nothing, but it might be useful."

"It was something she never would have missed before," I said. I shook my head. "But people miss moves all the time."

"But it concerned you?"

"I guess it did."

The nurse returned with Sarah, handed the doctor the chart.

"Okay, young lady, you sit up here and let's have a look at you."

"Have a look at you," she said. I was reminded of my father saying that it was all well and good for one to see a doctor, but the doctor had to see you as well. Here was my daughter, my Sarah, being seen by the doctor, and I stood by wishing that the doctor could not, would not see her at all. In the examination room, the very fear that had begun to push or jolt Meg and me close again now seemed to do just the opposite. It wasn't so much a coolness or estrangement as it was that we were dividing, cleaving our child; she wanted her daughter and I wanted mine. Even then, out of nervousness, I considered that word, *cleave*, and wondered how it could contradict itself so cleanly, wondered if the two meanings canceled each other out, leaving nothing in its wake. Cleave.

Dr. Gurewich had Sarah put her fingertips together, touch her nose, close one eye and then the other and take a pen, walk, hop, repeat series of syllables, repeat series of numbers, say the date, recall breakfast, recall yesterday, sing a song. The doctor looked at her eyes, felt her joints, tapped her reflex points with a hammer, checked her peripheral vision, talking all the while, a soothing voice, accent and all.

"Do you like television?" the doctor asked.

"I don't watch much."

"Spend much time on the computer?"

"I do my schoolwork on the computer."

"Do you watch videos and things like that?"

"Not so much."

"Do you like video games?"

"Not really. I used to play one when I was little. It was called *Turn Me Loose*."

"Was it a fun game?"

"I guess. I was six."

"I remember that game," Meg said.

"Does time ever seem to get away from you? You know, you're watching and then all of sudden it's time for bed or time to leave. Does that ever happen?"

"Sometimes. Is that bad?" Sarah asked.

The doctor shook her head. "Happens to all of us. Have you felt disoriented lately? Are you more forgetful?"

"I don't know."

"Ever forget where you are? Feel lost for a second or two?"

"No."

"This is going to sound like a strange question: Can you remember the last thing you forgot?"

Sarah laughed.

"I told you it was a weird question."

"I forgot I had a flute lesson."

"Ever done that before?"

"I can't remember."

That made me laugh. Meg shot me a glance.

"Very good," the doctor said.

The doctor went through many of the same tests again.

"Repeat after me: La fa ta."

"La fa ta."

"La la la fa ta ta."

"La la la fa ta ta."

"La la fa fa ta ta."

The incongruous, ironic part of the exam was that, though I was completely, absolutely invested in watching, though I was bothered by worry, agitated, and perhaps near panic, I actually experienced what might have been the kind of small seizure I was afraid my daughter had suffered through as I became aware that some minutes had passed without my regard. I came to or awoke to find the doctor holding a sheet of paper towel in front of my child's face. She was attempting to induce a seizure, I could see that, and I wanted to object but of course did not.

"Okay, Sarah, I'd like you to blow on the paper here and make it move. Do it until I tell you to stop. Big breaths."

Sarah followed the instructions. The paper towel moved away and fell back four times, eight, and then Sarah stopped blowing; her head dipped, she seemed to fall asleep, and her head cocked to the right.

"Sarah? Can you hear me? Red. Blue."

"Red?" Sarah asked.

"So you heard that."

"Mom?" Sarah looked to her mother.

"It's okay, baby."

"Everything's fine," Dr. Gurewich said. "I'd like to run an electroencephalogram. And we'll do the bloodwork. The seizures might be absolutely nothing. They could be environmental and might go away. It could be associated with her diet. I'd like you to chart everything Sarah eats for a week. And let's get rid of all perfumes, scented soaps, and shampoos. Is that okay, Sarah?"

Sarah nodded.

"What kind of science are you doing in school right now?"

"Biology."

"Any lab work? Dissecting anything? Any things that have a strong or disagreeable odor?"

"No lab at all."

"Good. Sarah, why don't you go out and wait in the other room. I want to schedule that test and talk to your parents about our next appointment." The doctor called the nurse and let her take Sarah down the hall.

"Well?" Meg said once the door was closed.

"Everything I told Sarah is completely true. But there is a possibility we're dealing with epilepsy."

"Oh my God," Meg said.

I thought it.

"It *might* be," Dr. Gurewich reiterated. "The good news about that is that even if it is epilepsy, drugs can control it. And epilepsy that shows in childhood does not mean a shortened life. If it is epilepsy, there will be drugs for the rest of her life." She paused to study our faces. "Let's do the tests and see what her blood tells us."

"What about the vision thing?" I asked.

"That could be caused by the seizures. They are very mild, and I'm sure she doesn't realize they're happening."

"That's why she didn't see my bishop?"

"Very likely. But we'll keep an eye on the vision problem."

The only good news you can hear when discussing your child's welfare is that there is absolutely, positively nothing wrong. Sarah's fear was palpable. She of course wanted to know what the doctor had said to us in private. I, of course, told her. Meg was unsure about whether to tell her; worse, she was uneasy. But anxiety was hardly her doing.

"The fact is, the doctor doesn't know what's wrong," I told her.

"She says you're fine," Meg said.

"The worst could be that you have to take some medicine," I said, quickly. "But she has to do the tests to figure out what medicine."

"Did I have a seizure?" Sarah asked.

"Maybe," I said. "It was a small one if you did."

"What is a seizure?"

I pulled the car over, parked under the shade of a chinaberry tree. I looked at Meg and she nodded to me.

"Is it really bad?" Sarah asked.

"No, slug, it's not really bad. Especially because we now know they're happening. It's as if you're taking a tiny nap. Like a little short circuit in your brain." (I was sorry I'd said "brain." I was sorry I'd said "short circuit.") "In a way we all have them from time to time. You're just having a few more."

"So, what does the doctor think I have?"

"She doesn't think anything yet. It could be your diet, your shampoo, or your deodorant," her mother said.

"I don't use deodorant."

"About that," I said.

"Zach," Meg complained.

But Sarah laughed.

Zenaida macroura. A left humerus from a pack rat nest and partial femur and proximal end of a tibiotarsus from the 20–25 cm level represents this resident species.

Without a lot of discussion, none at all, we deemed it best to behave as if there was little or nothing wrong. We were a family of idiots. Sarah went off to school the next day, a trouper, Meg held her office hours, and I went to campus and pretended to teach. Before class I stopped by the athletic center, what I grew up calling the gym, and tried to relieve some stress by knocking around a squash ball. A young Indian man I knew to be a graduate student in another of the sciences asked me if I wanted to play, and I politely told him no. I continued my punishment of the ball, attending to the sweet, startling silences between the bangs against the front wall and my racket.

"I'm pretty certain that ball is good and dead by now," someone behind me said, then coughed.

I turned to find Finley Huckster, that really was his name, standing on the other side of the plexiglass wall, a towel draped around his neck, wet from perspiration and drinking water from an old military canteen.

"And by dead I mean you killed it," he said. "What's got you so mad?"

"I'm not mad," I said. "At least, I'm not angry. Just trying to work up a decent sweat."

"I see."

"What are you doing here? Certainly you don't exercise."

"It's true that we English professors are not famous for our athletic prowess, but I am an exception."

"How is that?"

"I am exceptional."

I opened the door and ducked out to stand with him. We sat on the lowest level of the small bleachers. We stared at the empty court.

"How are you?" Finley asked.

"Tired."

"So, what do you think of our new dean?"

"We have a new dean?"

"Yes. Yearlong search. A thousand emails asking for our inconsequential input. You don't recall any of this?"

"Sounding a little familiar." I looked at his olive drab rubber canteen. "Why do you drink out of that thing?"

"It allows me to recall my Marine days. The rubber taste reminds me of how much I hated them."

"So, what's the new dean like?"

"She's a political scientist from Stanford. You know the type: Ivy bred, overachieving, no doubt *smarter* than the rest of us, or at least she thinks she is. You know, a dean." Finley offered me a pull on his canteen.

"No, thanks."

"And young. Very young. All the deans seem so young these days."

"Finley, it's not that they're that young. We're that old."

"That's true, but we ain't dead yet."

"Aye."

I taught my class, did a better job than I expected, considering that I essentially stood in front of them like a robot, opened my mouth, and let years of rehearsed lecture spill out without interest or passion. To my surprise, more students than not complimented me as they filed out.

"Great lecture, prof."

"Awesome lecture."

"Cool."

"Sick."

Grunt.

I then walked across campus. Clouds had gathered, but the sky was again making promises it couldn't keep. I dodged the bicycles and skateboards and made my way to my office, and there I waited for students that never showed up for my hours. This day one student did. It was Rachel Charles. She sort of sidled into the room.

"May I help you, Rachel?"

"I wanted to apologize," she said.

I remained in my chair, looked at her.

"About what happened out in the desert. I'm really sorry."

"Don't fret over it. Believe it or not, I was young once."

"I feel like such a fool. You must think of me as just a stupid little girl." Her words held some subtext that was simply not available to me.

"Okay. It's over now. Let's just move forward. Thank you for coming in and saying something."

"Is that your daughter?" She pointed a painted green nail at the photograph on the wall above my desk.

"Yes. Her name is Sarah. And that's my wife."

"She's beautiful."

I nodded.

"Professor Wells, I wasn't lying about my interest in geology," she said. "I have been trying to figure out what I'm interested in since I got to college."

"That's good."

"You really are inspiring to me."

"That's great. That's the sort of thing we professors like to hear." I waited for Rachel to make a move toward the door, but she didn't. I began to pack up my bag as if to leave. "You're doing well in the class."

"Thank you."

"Is there anything else?"

"I guess not."

I stood and put the strap of my bag over my shoulder. "Well, all right, then I'll see you on Thursday."

"Thursday."

I did not leave my office but sat back down. I was alone there, and so I did not trouble to straighten my shoulders. I felt weak as I realized I was quite obviously resisting going home. I wondered what that meant about me. However, that level of self-centered consciousness was quickly dislodged, was swept away in the stream of the present that was my daughter's situation.

The CBC and chemistry panel showed no anemia, no infections, no diabetes. "However," Dr. Gurewich said, "there are some vacuolated lymphocytes. That could mean one of several metabolic disorders, something as simple as an acid-base imbalance or some kind of malabsorption problem. The ophthalmologist's notes say that he saw what could be fluorescent deposits in the back of her eyes."

"What's that suggest?" Meg asked.

We were sitting in the doctor's private office at Children's Hospital. Her window looked out over a courtyard. I watched a woman push a child in a wheelchair. The child said something that made the woman laugh. I couldn't hear sounds but could see them, watched her sounds while I waited to hear Gurewich's response.

"It's too early to say. I've decided to schedule an electroretinogram. I know it seems like a lot, but I want to know everything."

Meg and I nodded.

"And we'll do a DNA analysis. So, we'll have to take a little more blood and a couple of tissue samples."

"What are you thinking?" I asked. "It sounds like you've got an idea of what this might be."

"Like I said, nothing yet. The EEG is probably near done now, so I'm going to go see Sarah. You can wait in here." She left.

Meg and I sat quietly for a few minutes. I looked at the things on and around Gurewich's desk. There was a basket with skeins of yarn and knitting needles on the floor.

"I wouldn't have taken Dr. Gurewich for a knitter," I said.

"What do you imagine she's thinking?" Meg asked.

"I have no idea."

"Aren't you scared?"

"I'm terrified," I said.

"You don't seem terrified."

"What are you talking about?" I asked.

"I mean I'm really upset, and you don't seem disturbed."

I shook my head. "What the hell are you talking about?"

She dabbed at the corners of her eyes with a tissue.

"I'm sorry my reaction isn't precisely like yours. However, you might just want to pull it together so that you don't make Sarah any more scared than she already is. What do you think?"

Meg said nothing.

I shook my head again. Then I realized I thought that she might have been looking for a fight in order to not think about what was happening. I didn't like it, but I had to admit that if true, it wasn't a bad strategy. I put my hand on her shoulder. "I am worried. I don't want to lose focus arguing over something like this."

Meg reached up and touched my hand.

I could tell she hadn't changed her mind about my reaction. I wanted to tell her that even in grief there had to be a diversity of form, just like with living organisms, but I didn't. Thinking about analogous bullshit was my way of dealing with stress, and there was no need for me to make things worse by airing any of it.

Sayornis nigricans. A completely preserved tarsometatarsus was recovered with ten other bones from the 18–20 cm level. These may have been from an owl pellet. The specimen, 16 mm long, is in the size range of a female. It was compared to *Sayornis saya*, which is larger, and *Contopus* and *Empidonax* spp., which is smaller.

4

There was mention of Naught's Cave in the journals of John Wesley Powell as he navigated the Colorado River. It was described as "but a mere cavity in the wall" that he observed but never explored, it being very likely that when he came upon it, there was no way to rest the boat while he investigated. It was more likely that he simply had no interest in entering it, it being "but a mere" cavity. No one knows why it came to be named Naught's Cave, there being no record of any member of his party going by that name. I suggested once that he meant the name literally, *naught* as in nothing. Nothing Cave. And so perhaps evidence of his lack of interest. For me, however, the cave held great interest, became my work, my focus, in some way my world. It was the one place that I knew more about than anyone else. I wondered if everyone needed such a place, if everyone could have such a place, if my daughter would ever have such a place.

Even when I was at home, Naught's Cave became a place where I hid from the rest of the world and life, my excuse being that I was working. My obsessive notes covered not only my desk but my person as well. Obsession was a trait that I employed conveniently, without much regard, but when employed it was earnest and complete, perhaps not quite the Platonic emulation of a desired quality, as that must have required an actual decision, but more a commitment born of simple weakness.

My mind was stranded amid piles of birds' bones in a pack rat midden in a tight, dank corner when I looked down to find my nineteen-month-old daughter turning blue. Half the paper label was peeled from a plastic water bottle but was nowhere in sight. Sarah was sitting in the shopping cart seat in the grocery market when it happened. I was standing by the cheeses. Meg came out of an aisle carrying a bag of rice when she saw my panic. She dropped the rice, the bag broke open, and rice slid and rolled and sprayed everywhere. My big clumsy fingers were in my daughter's mouth, and I was finding nothing.

"What's happening?" Meg asked.

"She ate paper."

I patted Sarah's back, then turned her over, held her upside down. She was not crying, and that was the most alarming part of all of it. Then suddenly she was crying. I breathed again. The wad of paper was out of her and between my fingers. Meg took the baby and glared at me.

"She peeled it off the bottle," I said.

"Weren't you watching her?"

That was Meg's way. She was a blamer; every bad thing had to be someone's fault. I hadn't saved our child from choking, but instead had only nearly killed her. I hadn't removed the paper, but had, in fact, put the foreign matter in her throat. I never considered that the child might tear the paper off the bottle and eat it. We had routinely given her plastic bottles just like this one to play with. I felt hollow, weak, guilty, and sick. That night I stood over her for more than an hour while she slept, watching her little back rise and fall with her breaths, making certain that she was still alive. It was my job, my only job in life, to keep this creature alive, to keep this little bird breathing.

The package was on the dining room table, a large envelope with a post office box return address in New Mexico.

Meg watched as I pulled out the shirt. "What is that?" she asked.

"It's a shirt," I said.

"I can see that. Is it used?"

"Pre-owned. Got it on eBay."

"You needed another shirt?"

"Not really," I admitted.

She made some kind of noise in her throat. I am sad to say I understood her completely. The shirt was just a shirt, and I was glad she had left the room as I was then alone to search its two flapped breast pockets. I was relieved and, oddly, a bit disappointed, even more strangely, discouraged, to find them empty. So, I had a new used shirt that looked enough like my old used shirts that I would no doubt slip it into the rotation. As I stuffed the garment back into the envelope, I felt a lump in the collar. There was a neatly folded note pinned, hidden, under the flap. I hesitated to unfold it as the hair on my neck stood up. Before I even read it, I knew I would not be telling Meg. I wondered if I would share it with anyone. Unfolded, the note read "Please Help to Us."

I felt every bit of the shirt to be sure there were no more notes. I looked at the envelope. The return address was a postal box and the zip code 87832. A quick check on my phone . . . Bingham, New Mexico.

All of this was just what it was: a distraction, whether welcome or not, from the terrifying situation at hand. The note was a strange affirmation of knowledge I did not have. It was easy to believe that someone was having me on. That was, in fact, more than likely, that I was the random target of some prank, perhaps one of a few or many targets. I knew absolutely nothing, but the notes were real, felt heavy in my hand, meaningful. This feeling, of course, fed my need to know something, anything at all, all the business with my child being nothing but questions. The nagging inquiry at the end of this red herring of a rainbow, though undeniably just another distraction, was epistemological. When rednecks get scared, they run to their guns. When intellectuals get scared, they run to fundamental philosophical problems: What is goodness? What is beauty? What is it to know a thing? About knowing, I was not so much interested in whether I could know some thing but in what kind of thing I could know. I knew that my cryptic notes were real, but I could not know what they meant, how they were meant, or whether they meant. I could not know whether my daughter would live into old age, but I could know what was making her ill, if only someone would tell me. Just as I could not know how a pile of bones could end up in pack rat middens in my cave, but I could know they were from a grebe.

That night Sarah cried out with a bad dream. Meg and I ran to her room the way we did when she had night terrors as a small child. She never awoke, as she never awoke then. Meg held her and rocked. I put my hand on Meg's shoulder, as if Sarah could or would feel my hand through another body. As I touched Meg, I felt her soften, and I felt close to her like I had so long ago. In that moment Sarah was not her daughter and my daughter but our daughter, the way she had been our daughter when we first brought her home, when looking at her was akin to looking at a portrait of the three of us. Meg looked at me, and I could see the fear.

"I'm scared too," I said.

While Meg took Sarah in to give blood for a DNA analysis, I went to campus. It was the day of the midterm exam, and though I wasn't teaching, I still had to be there to proctor the test and deal with whatever panic question six might cause. The campus was buzzing with news that some students were occupying the president's office. I read about it in the student rag while sitting in my office, regarded photos of the protesters sitting on the floor, staring at their phones and sipping from Starbucks cups. The students were apparently demanding many resignations because the president and his administration were insensitive to the needs of students of color. It sounded like my college days twenty-five years earlier, when we were asking for essentially the same things. I was sadly as apolitical then as I was at this moment. I dealt with fossils. I crawled through caves and measured the bones of birds long dead. The students had passed around a petition stating that the administration did not understand how profoundly they had been affected by the murder of a black teenager by police in Peoria, Illinois. The petition claimed that the students should not have to take exams, they were so distraught. A couple of black students came to my office, seeking me out as a black faculty member. I had never met either of them, a handsome man and a handsome woman, bright eyed and young, searching for intensity.

"Professor Wells?"

"Yes, I'm Wells."

"I'm Mya Chambers, and this is Daniel Johnson. I'm an English major," she said.

"History," Daniel said.

"We were wondering if you would join us, talk to us at a meeting tonight," Mya said.

"Who is 'us'?"

"The Students of Color Coalition," Daniel said. "We're protesting the lack of black faculty on campus."

"What do you want from me?"

"We want you to tell us how the university has systematically excluded people of color from becoming faculty." Mya looked at Daniel for approval.

Daniel nodded.

"So, it appears you already know what you want me to say," I said. This surprised them and, to tell the truth, me too. My tone suggested no patience at all. "You'd like me to say that this university has tried to keep black paleontologists from serving as professors here. Understand me—I know racism is real. I've been arrested a couple of times in Arizona for simply driving while black. I've been shot at by some white supremacists while on a dig and worried that the last words I might hear in life would be 'I got me one.' But I haven't personally experienced it here, though I'm certain there's some of it."

They stared at me as if I were on fire.

"For all I know I may not have gotten several grants because of racist panelists. I just don't know. I crawl into caves and find fossils and then identify them. I am a scientist. I should probably be more political in my thinking and dealings with the school. But I'm not."

Daniel appeared about ready to say something.

"I read in the school paper that you don't think you should have to take exams," I said. "It was an awful, terrible thing that happened back there in Peoria. I went to graduate school in Chicago. Do you know what the high school students in Peoria will be doing at the end of the term?"

"What?" Mya asked.

"Taking exams," I said. I had made them unhappy. They had no way of knowing that part of my rant was rooted in the fear and frustration generated by my daughter's undiagnosed illness.

"Protest is good," I said. I believe they thought I was about to make nice. "But if you want to do it, maybe you should march in the streets with people on the front line instead of doing the very American thing of ordering pizza and having a party on the floor of the president's office before you use your expensive educations to live good lives."

Daniel regained his footing. "So, you think there are enough black faculty on this campus?"

"There should be more," I said. "I don't disagree with you. But I don't have time to attend your party so I can feel good about myself. I really am a nerd who crawls around in caves. Maybe that's why I have a job here. I don't know." I paused to observe their reactions. I couldn't read much in their faces. Perhaps there was not much to read. Regardless, I was fairly shocked that I had said so much, especially because I cared so little. "Have I disappointed you?" I said, more rhetorically than anything else.

They said nothing, but it was clear they were quite ready to leave.

"I didn't mean to. I've had a long week."

They didn't know how to end our little encounter.

"You can go," I said, sounding harsher, sterner than I intended. I was, by all reports, a gruff man, though I believed I was merely direct. Directness, the last excuse of the curmudgeon, the grouch.

They walked away.

Hilary stepped sideways through my doorway. "Wow, you sort of laid into them, didn't you?"

"Did I?"

"You might get a reputation."

I shrugged. "Never had one. Might be fun."

"I doubt it."

"What do you want?" I asked.

"What's going on?" She studied me, half smiling, her head cocked to one side like a puzzled canine.

"Stuff at home," I said. I realized how that sounded. "My daughter is sick."

"I'm sorry to hear that."

"Yeah, me too."

"Come on, let me buy what passes for lunch around here."

I looked up at her from my chair and for a second simply didn't know who she was. I shook my head, but not as a response to her question, then said, "No, thank you." I added "Hilary" to satisfy myself that I knew who she was.

Eremophila alpestris. A humerus, complete, 22.7 mm in length, was found from the 19–25 cm level. This species has been reported from other Pleistocene deposits. The size is comparable to the races breeding today in the area.

Sarah and Meg were still at the hospital midafternoon. I got into my Jeep and drove over to join them, my heart racing the whole way. It was one of those Southern California days that people often said they hated, sunny and hot. I dismissed summarily the complaint, often from easterners, that the region offered no seasons. A rather unsophisticated lot, these complainers, at the very least lazy. Signs of seasons abounded in Los Angeles and around, more subtle than the abundant death of leaves that so many seemed so in love with. The blooming of flowers and trees, the appearance of various birds. In the spring, the phainopepla appeared, the males showing off their white-patched wings. Purple finches in the fall. Santa Ana winds blowing hot through October. Rains in the winter. The sun there was bright, often too bright, somehow too close, and it was so that day, hammering on me as I drove.

It irked me that Children's Hospital was so decidedly cheerful.

It irked me that I was irked by it. Why shouldn't the place have been cheerful? It was, after all, where most children got better. I should have believed that because of all the happy colors and tanks full of smiling fish and bright, shiny, floating balloons that my child would be made better as well. I wanted to believe that, but apparently I didn't. I had sunk into a pessimistic wormhole, and, knowing I couldn't extricate myself, I at least resolved to hide my fear.

I followed the red line on the floor to neurology. That unwavering, resolute red line. Situated between the blue and yellow lines, leading past the big fish tank, over the pedestrian bridge, having no meaning by its being red but meaning everything because it was red. I followed, chased, heeded the red line until it led me to my daughter.

Somehow my red line following got fouled up, and I arrived again at the big aquarium, where I stood staring at the oversized angelfish that decided to stare back at me. Something that Sarah had told me was called a black ghost slithered his eel body through my peripheral vision. I imagined that if I chose to hallucinate at that moment, the angelfish would speak to me, say something cryptic or profound; as I stood there entertaining this weird notion, it dawned on me that I was essentially hallucinating anyway. I looked down, rediscovered the red line, and set off again with neither more nor less resolve. This time I found Dr. Gurewich's office and my family.

Sarah embraced me as if she had not seen me in a very long while. It surprised me, scared me somewhat, though I loved the feeling of it, being reminded of when she was so much my baby. She had never felt smaller.

Dr. Gurewich called in a nurse. "Melissa, would you take Sarah and get her blood pressure, respiration, and heart rate?"

It was so clear that she was simply removing Sarah from the room that I became immediately terrified. Meg saw it in my eyes, and I saw it in hers.

"We'll be right here, baby," Meg said to Sarah.

The nurse led her away and closed the door.

Gurewich's eyes looked tired. She rubbed her forehead and temples and appeared to be not all there.

"Were you up late?" I asked her.

She absently reached into her knitting basket and pulled a skein of blue yarn onto her desk. "No," she said. She paused and kneaded the yarn with her hand. "Sometimes I get migraines."

I nodded. "What have you learned?"

"That scents often bring them on," she said.

"About Sarah," I said.

"Of course." The doctor collected herself.

"What is it?" Meg asked.

"I first became suspicious when Sarah's urine tests showed dolichol. So we took a closer look and did find vacuolated lymphocytes. Those are white blood cells that have holes in them."

"Okay," I said.

"There is a group of disorders called neural ceroid lipofuscinoses. NCL."

"Okay."

"I believe—I strongly believe—that Sarah has Batten disease. That would explain all of her symptoms. Her skin and tissue samples support this diagnosis." Gurewich kneaded her yarn.

"How do we treat it?" I asked.

Meg was silent.

"We can't," Gurewich said.

"You mean she'll just live with it, have these seizures? Can we control the seizures?" I asked.

Gurewich leaned even more forward. "There is nothing we can do."

"Excuse me?" I said.

"What are you talking about?" Meg asked. "What are you saying?" She stood up and sat right back down.

I took Meg's hand.

"The DNA analysis shows a mutation in the CLN3 gene on chromosome sixteen."

"Are you saying that one of us gave our child this?" Meg said.

"It's a recessive trait. It comes from both of you. You are both what we call unaffected carriers. There would have been no way for you to know."

Meg pushed my hand away, gently, but away, ostensibly to find a tissue in her bag.

Empidonax sp. A right humerus with a damaged head was taken from the 20–25 cm level. Too few properly prepared reference specimens of the various species were available to make accurate species determination. The characters of the subfossil appear nearer *E. hammondii* than *E. difficilis*, but it is closer to the latter in size.

There was no other way to say it, except of course that we were left to say it ourselves, though not out loud; that would have been too much. Our daughter was dying. My little Sarah would not survive this genetic defect. I was lost. Meg was lost. She couldn't even blame me for what was happening. For her sake, I wished that she could have.

Over time, my daughter would suffer worsening seizures, her sight would finally fail altogether, her speech and motor skills would grow progressively worse and fade, and she would suffer mental impairment; she would become demented. I would lose her before she was gone. Selfishly, my first impulse was to find the cheap, old, five-shot .38 that had once been my father's but was now hidden away in a trunk, put the muzzle inside my dry mouth, and pull the trigger. My usual response to all situations (namely, to search for and implement a solution) had been effectively taken away. There was no solution. Even the quickest study of the disease left no room for doubt. My daughter would not be cured; her life would not be made better in what abbreviated time remained for her. And worst of all, worst of all, my daughter was all too capable at that moment of understanding the gravity of her situation. How does a parent tell his daughter that she will not only die young but that she will essentially fall apart on her way to her end? Does a father tell his daughter? I looked at Meg. I wondered if she would be able tell her daughter, my daughter, our daughter.

We did not tell her that night. We told her that the doctor thought she had epilepsy, that she had to determine what kind of medication she would take, that we believed everything would be all right, that she would live a long life. Our lie was made okay because we left ourselves an out: we had said we believed she would be well, not that we knew, not that it was a fact, not that it was true. Belief was a wonderfully plastic notion. We put her into bed and tucked her in, as we did when she was two, warm under her blanket and our lie.

In the dining room we sat and did not speak. I could think of nothing to say. I couldn't imagine what Meg might say. What amazed me was that I did not let my mind wander to my work, my usual refuge, distraction, safe harbor. I would not be sleeping. Meg and I needed space at that moment, not each other. Correct or not, that was my reading.

"I need to think," I said. I left the house.

Castling Short

And so the world was different. I drove from my house on that
Thursday night through the busy place that was Old Town Pasadena,
a sweet and glittery advertisement for wholesome American night-
life. Everyone appeared so light and carefree, floating along, laughing, feeling safe. I continued south on the 110 to downtown, to a
restaurant bar on Main Street just a block away from skid row, a
place that I had heard mentioned on campus by a few grad students,
named, quite understandably, the Bar on Main Street. Downtown
Los Angeles was making its way back to presentability but still
wore the grime and dirt I needed at that moment. I didn't really
remember just how to drink stupidly, but I imagined it would not
be difficult to figure out. The door was in the shape of a big key-
hole, and I surprisingly fit right through it. Strangely, since I had
heard some students mention the place, but not so strangely from
the overall look and tenor of the joint, there were, in fact, no students inside, just a bunch of rough men and a couple of women who
looked even rougher. The bartender, a short man with only half a
mustache, asked me what I wanted.

He caught me staring at his lip. "I lost a bet," he said. "What do
you want?"

"Scotch," I told him.

"What kind?"

"Any kind," I said.

"Cutty Sark?"

"Sure."

"Ice?"

"No."

"Water?"

"Just the scotch."

I looked at the door, perhaps hoping for a familiar face to enter, perhaps just because it was the door and the way out. My drink was delivered and I downed some. The whisky burned my throat and made my eyes well up. I coughed. Actually, I gagged.

A guy a couple of stools over laughed at me. I didn't mind. He was about my size but wanted to seem larger in his leather jacket, which maybe wasn't such a bad thing in a place like this. "Go easy there, tough guy," he said. "Jimmy, give the man some water," he called to the bartender.

"Thank you," I said to the bartender and then to the man down the bar. I drank some water, then tried another sip of whisky.

"And my name's not Jimmy," the bartender said.

"Whatever."

I drank the rest of the scotch and tapped the bar for Half Mustache to bring me another one.

To my dismay, Leather Jacket moved clumsily over the couple of stools and sat on the one next to me. "I don't care what the fuck he says, his name is Jimmy. My name is James, what's yours?"

"So you're both Jimmys."

"What? No, I'm James."

"Zach."

"Lost?" he asked.

"No. Why?"

The bartender put another scotch in front of me and made a point of sneering at James.

James ignored the bartender. "There are only a couple of reasons to be in this shithole. One, you're already drunk and want to get drunker. Two, you ain't drunk and want to get drunk and this is where you usually come to get drunk. Three, you're lost. You ain't drunk. I've never seen you in here before. So, or ergo, you're lost."

"Nice reasoning," I said.

"It's a gift." He took a long pull on his bottle of beer, which I believed to be a Pabst. "Also a curse."

"How so?"

"I can always talk myself into having another drink."

"I see."

"So what do you do?"

"I'm an intrepid explorer, a dinosaur hunter."

James laughed loudly and slapped my shoulder with a floppy hand in an exaggerated way that revealed some kind of insecurity and made me not trust him. Not that I would have trusted him anyway

"What about you?"

"Between jobs. It's rough out there."

I nodded. My nod was sincere, as "out there" for me meant the world of my daughter. I looked around the bar. A couple of men were now playing pool. I sort of wanted to play also, but I was a bit afraid of the place. I think James sensed this.

"I had me a good job for a while," he said. "I used to drive a truck for Ralphs. Then I got sent up for a bit. I don't care what anybody says, nobody out here will cut an ex-con any slack. Know what I mean?"

"I can only imagine. Why were you in jail?"

"Prison," he corrected me.

"Prison."

"They said I stole some stuff. You know, everybody says it, but I really didn't do it. Only thing I ever stole in my life was a box of Mr. Bubble when I was eight."

"Mr. Bubble."

"I had a thing about bubble baths."

"Who doesn't like a bubble bath?" I said.

"I know, right? So, where do you work?"

This whole thing was going south fast. "I work at the university."

"No shit," James said. He ran his fingers through his greasy hair. "What do you do over there?"

"I'm a technician in a lab."

"No shit. Pay pretty good?"

"Pays shit," I said. "I'm looking for something else. What about you, what's the last job you had?" I was attempting to redirect the focus of the conversation back to him. I had read that was a good thing to do.

"What kind of lab?"

I knew better than to say anything that suggested medicine, chemistry, or something that might have suggested the presence of chemicals or drugs. I felt rather clever making that connection. "A physics lab," I said. "I set up experiments for the students."

The disappointment was clear on his face.

A noisy, skinny little man came into the bar. He was small, but he had a big presence. He yelled at James right off. "Hey, James, you're a fat pig and you snore even when you're awake."

"Yeah, well, fuck you very much," James said. James smiled at me. "That there's Derrick."

Derrick moved to the bar and talked to a woman.

"Your friend?"

"Yeah, I guess you could say that."

"Well, I'll let you visit with him. I have to go home." I knocked back my second shot. I called for the bartender. "What do I owe you?"

"Don't go yet. Meet Derrick." James called to his friend. "Derrick, get your ass over here and meet my friend Zach."

Derrick left the woman he was talking to and came over. He reached out and shook my hand. "I'm Derrick."

"Zach here works at the university," James said.

"What, are you a professor?" Derrick laughed.

"Works in a lab," James said.

"Oh yeah? What kind of lab?" Derrick asked.

"Physics."

"You work with all them oscilloscopes and shit like that?" Derrick was pleased with himself.

"Sometimes."

Derrick gave a surreptitious look around. "You like coke?"

"No," I said. "Listen, I'd better be leaving."

"Stay," Derrick said.

"Come on, Zach."

"You know what the difference between acid and coke is?" Derrick asked. "Like anybody does acid anymore. Know what the difference is?"

I shook my head.

Derrick was laughing a stupid laugh. "With acid, you see God. When you do coke, man, you are God."

"That's pretty funny. I really have to go."

"Come on," James said again and grabbed my sleeve.

I said, "Let go of my arm."

"It doesn't have to be like that," Derrick said. James did not let go of my arm. Somewhere in the cellular memory of my muscles was three years of Marine training. Without thinking but wanting to, I grabbed James by the index finger, bent it backward, and broke him down to a knee. I then punched the small man in the throat, sent him to hug the nearest stool. I tossed some money on the bar, let James go, and started out. James started after me, and I turned to face him. I remembered something that a friend told me once, that nobody enters a fight they don't believe they can win. The man backed away.

I got into my Jeep and drove a couple of blocks away and parked, collected myself, convinced myself that I was not drunk. I was embarrassed but not unhappy. Then I drove home.

I arrived home to find Meg in bed, either sleeping or pretending to sleep. I sat in the big chair in the corner and looked out the window, still dressed and wearing my boots, though I did trouble to brush my teeth so I wouldn't smell like the cheap whisky that sadly had had no effect on me.

After about ten minutes, Meg said, "I'm not asleep."

"I think we should tell Sarah everything," I said.

Meg did not lift her head from her pillow. "I disagree."

I knew she would. I knew she would not only because I understood the argument for not telling the child but also because I imagined that she would disagree with whichever way I chose to proceed. Whether it was simply a matter of playing devil's advocate to promote helpful discussion or just contrariness, I didn't know. And I really didn't care.

"You think we should lie to her," I said.

Meg sat up. "I think we simply don't tell her."

"Then what do we tell her?"

She lay back down. There would be no more discussion that night, and nothing had been decided. I didn't want to lie to my daughter, but neither could I imagine telling her the truth. Of course, that was the stuff of it, not whether we would tell her the truth about her disease but could we. I thought to apologize to Meg, but instead I continued to sit and stare numbly out the window at the dark outline of the hills.

Duck Duck Goose. Sarah used to love that game. She never minded being the goose. It was always fun with a great many kids, she told me. I felt now as if I were playing the game all alone. The ducks, the goose, and It, chasing myself back to where I started and remaining It because I could not reach myself before I fell back into my seat.

While Meg slept, I looked up the return policy of the vendor who had sold me the shirt. Simple enough. I would mail back the garment with a note stating the problem, and they would send me another shirt or give me a refund. I wrote a brief letter explaining that the shirt was too tight, that I would need an extra-large, that the color didn't matter. Under the flap of the collar, I hid a smaller piece of paper and on it I wrote, "¿Que puedo nacer para ayudar?" It all felt rather stupid, certainly pointless, but I was compelled to do it.

Nf3 b6

That morning, without having slept, I made breakfast and had it waiting for Meg and Sarah when they woke. Sarah would be going to school. We'd decided that the day before. They sat at the table and stared at my back while I flipped pancakes. "Let me ask you guys this," I said. "Is there a difference between flapjacks and pancakes?"

"Flapjacks?" Sarah had never heard the word.

"Yeah, flapjacks. That what some people call them. Or used to." I made a show of flipping a cake. "There's even something called johnnycakes."

"What are they made of?" Sarah asked.

"Johnny, I suppose."

The girl laughed.

"What about a game of chess this afternoon?"

"Okay."

It was clear that neither Meg nor I were going to broach the subject of Sarah's illness this morning. It was tacit but clear, transpicuous. It felt good not to talk about it. The failure to address the topic also made me feel weak. That was fine, I thought, thinking that evidently, in this regard, I was weak.

I drove Sarah to school. We didn't say much, but it was all very like any other morning. She fiddled with the radio, complained about the music of her generation, ridiculed the music of mine, and settled on the classical station.

"I hate Vivaldi," she said.

"Everyone hates Vivaldi, but no one will admit it."

"Queen pawn to d4," she said. "That's my opening move. I want you thinking about that."

"You love messing with me."

"It's so easy." She looked out her window. "Most underrated rock band."

"The Monkees," I said. "Most overrated rock band."

"The Beatles," she said.

"Most overrated painter."

"Georgia O'Keeffe," she said.

"Really?"

"Flat."

"Most overrated novel?" I asked.

Together we said, "*Infinite Jest.*"

"Still, I'm sorry he's dead," Sarah said.

We didn't say anything else during the short balance of the drive. I let her out, watched her merge into the stream and disappear through the door, all the while feeling like the liar that I actually was.

c4 e6

Finley Huckster was my age, but though I had no doubt he was in better shape than I was, he looked considerably older. Still, we were fairly evenly matched on the squash court. The play was good for me up to a point, and then depression overtook me again. Huckster noticed.

"You want to talk about it?" he asked.

"My daughter is dying," I said, flatly.

"I didn't expect that," he said and fell silent.

That was the first time I had said it out loud to anyone. I cannot say that it felt bad or good, but I felt somehow stronger.

"How is she?" Huckster asked. "You know what I mean."

"She's not suffering." I could tell that he didn't know whether it was appropriate to ask what was killing her. "It's a neurological disease. Batten disease. I'd never heard of it either. I wish it was good old-fashioned epilepsy."

"What's to be done for it?"

"Apparently nothing. We'll get the customary second and third opinions, but I trust this doctor. Sadly."

"So, what now?"

I didn't want to and so did not go into the details of my child's forthcoming diminution, but he was asking a very good question. "I haven't thought that far," I said. "We're told she has a few years. She's always wanted to go to Paris."

Huckster raised his brows and nodded.

It was a good idea. Meg would like it. Sarah could have the trip while she was still with us, cogent enough to enjoy it. "Thank you, Finley."

I don't think Huckster knew why I was thanking him, but he said, "Of course, that's what we humanities types are good for. Family advice and five-year plans, those are our specialties. I like to include reference to the next five-year plan in the current one. Art, my boy."

Nc3 Bb7

I took a guiltily long shower. The steam was serving to clear not only my sinuses but my thinking as well. Huckster was already dressed by the time I came back to my locker.

"Zach, I'm really sorry about your daughter."

I nodded.

"Who knows, perhaps someone will come up with a treatment in the next couple of years."

"Thanks, Finley."

In my office I did what I always did in my office, which was basically nothing. I kicked my feet onto my desk and looked out the window at the skyline of Los Angeles, tried not to think; in other words, I tried even more aggressively to do absolutely nothing. Then I noticed Hilary's folder under my boots. I picked it up, opened it, started to read.

It was hardly raw data. I did not work in Hilary's field, but I could understand it. I could not assess whether her work was cutting edge, new, or derivative, but I could say that it was clearly written and compelling. Her work focused not on the predictability of earthquakes but on the predictability of frequency and strength of aftershocks given location, depth, and strength of the initial quake. It seemed to me that the work was solid and ready to be sent out. I was confused.

I shouted out, "Hilary! Professor Gill!" I looked out my open door and saw a passing graduate student. "Is Professor Gill's door open?"

He looked. "Yes."

I got up and marched down the hall, stood at her doorway. "Did you not hear me shouting your name?"

"I did not," she said. She was sitting at her desk, reading exams.

"I was looking at your so-called raw data."

I could see her tighten.

"This is not raw. Obviously, I don't know what the hell is going on here, but why haven't you sent this out?"

"What?"

I stepped inside and closed her door. "I don't know what you're thinking, but this appears to be good and fairly polished work. I'm confused. I thought this was going to be a bunch of meaningless numbers. It is not meaningless numbers."

"You like it?"

"It doesn't matter whether I like it. What is this approval you keep looking for?" I was sounding harsh, but I didn't care. She wouldn't have believed me if I hadn't been harsh. "I want you to send this out right away. Don't ask me where. Talk to Flint. It's his area. Has he seen this?"

"No."

"Show this to him. Please, show it to him." I dropped the folder on her desk with a loud plop. "I'll go have a word with the chair." I walked out, muttering. I thought the muttering was a nice touch.

Bg5 Bb4

Odd for a paleontologist, my having to deal necessarily with not only the past but the distant, fossilized past. My philosophical method in most situations was to proceed without any consideration of the past, to forget the history of the problem, to forget all that came before, and to operate solely by investigating what facts were present at the time. I didn't care that Hilary Gill might have been seen as pissing away her six years of tenure clock. I didn't care that she, for whatever reasons, had sabotaged herself. I cared only that a scientist down the hall from me was making good work. Fuck clocks.

I went directly to Mitch Rosenthal's office. "I understand that you're the chair of this carnival."

"For a while, anyway." Mitch was a petroleum geologist, more suited for Exxon than academe. Though he was decent enough, he was no overachiever, though he could be a stickler.

"I just looked at Hilary Gill's research."

"It's sort of a done deal, don't you think?"

"I don't think," I said. "She's made some good work. It's not just the raw data she advertises. She's going to take it to Flint. He'll know what to do for her."

"She's done nothing in the past six years."

"Apparently, that's not true. The work didn't come out of thin air. I don't know why she kept it to herself. Maybe dudes like us scare the hell out of her or some shit. I really don't care. You need to go to bat for her."

Rosenthal twisted his fat ass in his fatass chair and embarrassed himself with a fatass sound. "I don't know."

I was getting angry. Of course, I had come into his office fully prepared to be angry. "If you won't go to the dean, then I will. Flint will go with me."

"You've talked to him?"

"No, but I know him. He's got these things that hang down between his legs. I think they're called balls."

"I'll talk to the dean."

"She needs a little more time," I said.

"Okay, I'll talk to her."

I left Rosenthal's office feeling a little like I had felt when fleeing the bar the previous evening, though this time I felt a little more like a bully. I didn't feel bad about it.

e3 h6

Someplace along the way, philosophers (a troublesome tedious lot at best) strangely decided that we cannot directly perceive things— the material world, sidewalks, carpets, rivers—but only our ideas of these things. This was a move in thinking that happened quite casually, without proof, as is the wont of such people. Would that their assertion were true, then I would not be experiencing my daughter directly, but only the idea of my daughter and so only the idea of the condition that would kill her. If that were true, then I could manipulate my idea as I might a dream, change the world around me. Just a little thinking dismisses the idea of sense data. Where do the ideas come from? Is an idea real? Is there anything between the idea and my perception of it? This is what I was thinking about as I placed the chess pieces on the board.

Sarah was just home from school, in good spirits, though not cheery. She was eager to play our game. She always enjoyed reducing me to a king scampering hopelessly around the board.

"I see you've changed clothes," I said to her as she took the seat across from me at the little table in the den.

"One needs loose-fitting clothes for close fighting."

"Where'd you get that bit of wisdom?"

"From you." Sarah made the first move. d4

I moved my knight. Nf6

After a couple of moves. "How was school?" I asked.

"School was school." Bh4. "How was school?"

"School was school," I said. c5

Meg walked into the room with a stack of papers.

"I see Mom brought school home with her," I said.

"I am afraid that is true," she said.

"Should we tell her?" I asked.

"Tell me what?" Sarah asked.

"You do it," I said to Meg.

"Your father and I have only talked about it briefly, but how would you like to take a trip to Paris?"

"Paris? Are you joking?"

"No."

Bd3

Bxc3

"I think we could all use a vacation," I said. "A nice big vacation." I looked at her face. She appeared genuinely excited, but it was muted. "Does that sound good?"

"Are you two playing while we talk about this?" Meg asked.

"No," Sarah said. "We wouldn't dream of it."

"I hate both of you," Meg said. "I have half a mind to read some of these poems to you. That'll teach you."

"Okay, we give up," I said.

"Paris," Sarah said. "Thank you." She got up and hugged her mother. She then came to me.

"You might want to take that hug back after you see my next move." d6

"Oh my," she said in mock surprise. Then, as if she had it all planned, she castled short. 0-0. She smiled but did not look at me.

"Your daughter is a demon," I said to Meg.

"Oh, I know."

"A demon," I repeated, looking at Sarah's beautiful face. "She is not kind to her poor old father."

"War is hell," she said. "Do you know why I always beat you, Daddy?"

"Tell me."

"Because you hate to lose pieces."

"Is that so?"

"You can't protect everybody. You just have to get the better of it or get the position you want."

"Yes, ma'am." Nbd7

All those bones in that cave. Stories in those bones, in the pack rat middens, in the layers. Were they stories if they happened to creatures that don't tell stories? I wondered if the memories of birds were stories. Did things happen to birds they knew? I could not forensically determine the cause of death of any of the birds I had found. I knew nothing about them except their ages and that I assumed that they looked like other birds of the same species, all speculation, induction, perhaps desire to believe that I knew something about their world, if not my own.

Nd2 Qc7

"Where are you going?" Meg asked.

"Campus. I thought I'd work in my office for a while," I said.

"You never work there."

"I'm going to start trying. Campus is nice at night when no one is around. There's some stuff I need to do in the lab too."

"Are we going to be okay?" Meg asked.

I was at the door, my hand on the knob. "I don't know," I said. "I'm just so lost right now."

"Me too."

"I'm sorry," I said.

"About what?"

"That you have to live through this."

Meg didn't respond to that. "Sarah is excited about Paris. That was a good idea. Maybe it will be good for us too."

"Maybe."

"How long will you be out?"

"Not long," I said, though I didn't know what I was telling her. The truth was, I had no idea how to work in my campus office. There was actually nothing for me to do in the lab, my being uncharacteristically caught up. I was lying to my wife. I was headed out to a bar near campus. I had no idea why, except that I had to be someplace.

Qc2 g5

The tavern was called Study Hall. It was a lively place, though hardly studious, in a neighborhood that had once been considered bad but was now acknowledged as *up and coming*, a gentle way of saying "still bad," *bad* being a relative term meaning "white youth at risk." It had always been my theory that a student was more likely to get ripped off by a fellow student than by a person on the street. Regardless, I was there, parked off a side street a few blocks away. Several screens showed various sporting events involving different balls and uniforms. Students, graduate and undergraduate, were by turns animated and deadpan. Panpsychism, the view that consciousness is everywhere, was fairly debunked by the scene. Despite my snarky take on the whole scene, what I was taken with, why I was there, was that these people were alive. I was not certain that I was.

I found a booth and sat, half watched a football game on one of the overhead screens. I looked at the kids in the tavern and realized my daughter would never make it to this stage of her life. I once talked to a man who had lost his son as a child. He told me that every year on the boy's birthday he wondered what he might have been like, what he might be doing. It was very sad. Here I was imagining somewhat the same while my daughter was still alive.

Sarah was no prodigy, if in fact there is such a thing, when it came to chess. I taught her the game when she was seven, and like any other seven-year-old, or any new player for that matter, she simply had fun with the way the pieces moved. Of course, there was a special fascination with the knight. She played just the way I played then and would years later, even while she grew as a player. She realized that there was much to know and began reading about the game, studying. By the time she was nine, she understood chess far better than I ever had. I did progress, only by proximity and a desire to offer her at least a small challenge. By the time she was eleven, I often had the feeling she was going easy on her old man. It didn't come easily to her. She worked hard, and that was what impressed me so, her tenacity, *obsessiveness* being such a packed word, but of course it was just that, a function of a sharp, open, restive mind. She never talked about her study, her knowledge, never claimed or announced that she would be using this opening or employing that defense, but instead played to merely watch them work. And perhaps so that she could laugh just a bit at me. It saddened me that her tenacity could not help her now. People are wont to speak of people as fighters in the face of terminal illness, and maybe they are, but terminal without hope is terminal. Without hope. There is nothing to fight. It is like fighting time. Don Quixote. Would that my daughter could have clawed her way back or that I could have rescued her, but no such thing was possible. This thinking consumed me, was always with me, and it not only threatened to, but did pull me down to a dark place, a place that I secretly began to recognize as a safe harbor.

Bg3 h5

I could feel myself slipping, from what to where I had no idea. To say that I felt lost is inaccurate only because it is stated with real ignorance of my feelings. Every time I felt that self-indulgent self-pity, I reminded myself for whom death had come, would be coming. My sadness didn't mean a thing, my pain was meaningless, and so I had no idea what to feel or what to do. Not an unusual condition for me, but instead of customary awkwardness, all I felt was needy or something like need, a burning of sorts.

"Professor Wells?" It was Rachel Charles. She held a blue drink with a red umbrella. "I'm shocked to see you in here."

"Me too, frankly," I said. We looked around, awkwardly. "Colorful drink."

"Yeah, isn't it? It's called a Tornado."

"Is it?"

"Is it what?"

"A tornado."

"I guess. It's not really that strong. I don't think anything here is that strong." She glanced up at a screen, then back at me. "May I join you?"

I took a deep breath, but I didn't survey my surroundings. I nodded. Rachel sat across from me in the booth. "I can't believe you're in here."

"I like the occasional beer just like anyone else. And it's Friday."

"To Fridays." She raised her glass.

I touched the neck of my bottle to it. "Are you in here often?"

"Not that often. My friends are over there."

I didn't look.

"What are you doing here?" she asked. She made a show of letting down her hair.

"Well, I'm not looking for rocks," I said.

She laughed.

"So, what did I say to get you so interested in geology?"

"I don't know. Just the way you talk about it."

This was amazing to me since I knew I taught that class asleep on my feet. "Really? That pleases me."

After another long silence during which we both stared up at the screen, Rachel asked, "Do you dream in color?"

"Excuse me?"

"Do you dream in color?"

"I think everybody dreams in color," I told her.

"Why do you say that?"

"I say that because before the mid-nineteenth century and the invention of photography, no one ever thought about anything being in black and white. There was no concept of the world being anything but color."

"That makes sense," she said. The way she said this made me think she at least believed she dreamed in black and white.

"Of course, that's just my theory."

"It makes sense."

My phone rang. I excused myself and answered. It was my wife. "I'm on campus," I told her. "Wait, what's wrong?" She told me that something was wrong with Sarah. "What is it?"

"I think she's having a seizure."

"Dial 911. I'm on my way."

I looked at Rachel. "Emergency."

"I hope everything is okay," she said after me.

The very strange thing that happened to me during my drive home was that the world turned to black and white. There were no flashing lights in front of my house and that confused me. I rushed inside to find Meg standing in the kitchen.

"Where's Sarah?" I asked.

"The seizure stopped. She came out of it. I never called the paramedics."

"Was it a bad one?"

"It was like the one in the doctor's office, except it lasted longer and she looked more out of it. She wasn't convulsing or anything like that." It was clear that Meg was shaken. I put my arm around her but couldn't find any words.

We sat at the table.

"Tea?" she asked.

"I'll get it," I said. I got up and took the kettle to the faucet. "I'm glad you didn't call the paramedics. That would have just scared her unnecessarily, I think."

"Yes. Where were you?"

"I was in my office, but I was on my way to my car when you called." I put the kettle on the stove and set the flame.

"Sounded like you were in a bar."

"I was outside of one. I was parked near Study Hall." I walked into the kitchen and poured myself a glass of water from the tap. "Did she say anything? Was she aware of what happened?"

"I don't really know. I don't think so."

"How could this happen?" I asked. "She's always been so healthy."

There was of course nothing more to say, and so Meg said nothing. And I said nothing more. She retired to the shower to nurse her fear. I moved to the study and found myself staring numbly at the notes I had received through my eBay purchases. The notes had slipped my mind, but now they were again in front of me, bothering me. I wondered how long before my shirt would be sent again, what the hidden note would say, if there would be a note.

Be4 h4

I walked into Sarah's room and looked at her. Her sleep breathing appeared so normal. I wondered whether her dreams were her own, the kinds, the ones she was used to, or if they were tortured and confused. Her face looked peaceful enough; I couldn't believe how beautiful she was. It occurred to me that I was actually in a dream. How I knew that, why I thought that, was unclear, as none of the usual dream markers were present. But it was a dream, and in it I became terrified, because why would I dream such a mundane, ordinary, normal thing unless in the real, waking world I would find the dream contradicted? When I awoke, would I find my daughter without breath, without light? And then

I calmed myself, thinking that perhaps she was not asleep at all but pretending, so as to please me. I awoke and found the diffused light of daybreak at the window and my daughter standing at my bedside.

"Daddy, I'm scared," she said.

I lifted the covers and let her get into the bed beside me, her body against mine as it hadn't been in so long, since she'd gotten older and such contact was inappropriate or creepy. I held her close and she was four years old again, and at four she was not dying.

Holding her like that, close like that, we fell asleep and I did not dream.

Still, we awoke early enough to not feel rushed in our preparation for the day. I made pancakes while Meg squeezed oranges and Sarah tried to get us interested in local news stories in the paper.

"There was a bear in La Cañada," she said. "It came down and got into somebody's pool."

"That's why we don't have a pool," I said.

"We're close to the mountains. Why don't we get a bear?" Sarah sipped from the glass of juice Meg put in front of her.

"Be careful what you wish for," Meg said.

We fell into an awkward silence.

"Maybe a mountain lion on your birthday," I said.

"That would be nice," Sarah said.

I put a plate of pancakes on the table. "Screw school," I said.

"What?" Meg said.

"We're going for a hike up the mountain this morning," I said.

Meg handed me a glass of juice. "Zach."

"What?"

"You teach today."

"I have a sudden cold." I faked a cough. "I wouldn't want to get the kiddies sick." I looked at Sarah. "You look a little feverish."

"Skip school?"

"You don't want to pass it on, do you?"

"Mom, will you go?" Sarah asked.

"You two have a good time."

Meg gave me a look I could not read.

Our established trail was less than half a mile from our back door. It was not much used, partly because it was hidden and not well known, but also because it was not maintained and could be steep and rough in patches. The trail was a trial, my poet wife said just before swearing off the path for good. Had we not grown up with the trail, had we not come to know it so intimately, I doubt we would have used it. As it was, we viewed it as more or less ours, something the two of us shared. The route became indistinct enough in several spots that if unfamiliar, a bit of orienteering was required. For us, it was just a walk in the park. We were on a track that saw little enough human traffic that we occasionally came upon bear or cougar scat or other signs, though we had never seen either. Still, we were sure to make plenty of noise as we traveled.

I walked uphill behind my daughter. I studied her gait, her big feet landing deliberately, one foot firmly planted before the second moved. Patches of fog hung in the trees above us. As when she was much younger, Sarah wondered aloud whether we could climb into the fog and clear it away like cobwebs.

About a mile into the hike we came upon a pile of scat. We knelt beside it and gave it a look. There was plenty of hair in it.

"Too big for a coyote," Sarah said.

I nodded. "Whatever it was tried to cover it."

"A cat?" she asked.

"I think so."

Sarah looked around.

I touched the shit with my finger. It was still warm.

"Yuck," Sarah said.

"It's only shit," I said.

Sarah laughed.

"It's just a word. A very versatile word. Even though we know this is shit, and we've just found this shit, we can still say, 'What is this shit?' By the way, this shit is very warm."

"What's that mean?"

"It means it's not that old," I said in a loud voice.

I could sense Sarah's alarm.

"Don't worry," I told her. "We just want to be sure that we're heard. They're more afraid of us than we are of them."

"I don't think that's true," Sarah said.

"Well, don't worry anyway. Want to head back?"

"No way."

"That's my girl."

We continued on. "Let's sing."

"Sing what?"

"What about 'Lydia.' From the Marx Brothers movie. Lydia, oh Lydia, that encyclopedia, queen of the tattooed ladies."

We sang.

> Lydia, oh Lydia, say have you met Lydia?
> Oh Lydia, the tattooed lady.
> She has eyes that folks adore so
> And a torso even more so.
> Lydia, oh Lydia, that encyclopedia.
> Oh Lydia, the queen of tattoo.
> On her back is the battle of Waterloo
> Beside it the Wreck of the Hesperus too
> And proudly above waves the red, white, and blue.
> You can learn a lot from Lydia.

"Why do you know that song?" Sarah asked.

"*At the Circus* was my favorite movie when I was a kid."

"I like it too."

"Watch the ridge over there. Maybe we can get a distant peek. Maybe see the white tip of its tail."

"Why didn't you name me Lydia?"

"Good question. We liked the name Sarah better."

"And it was Grandma's name."

"There was that."

We walked on another quarter mile. I asked Sarah how she was holding up, and she said she was fine. "A lot of people say that we have no seasons. That's because they don't look. Look around. These are our autumn colors. Look at the ochre of the redshank on that slope. And the buckwheat is that rusty color, not as dark as the brown of the laurel sumac."

Sarah studied the landscape.

"The world is around us. It's always changing. Sometimes it takes millions of years to see it. Sometimes seconds."

"Us too?" Sarah asked.

"Us too."

Bxb7 Qxb7
Bxd6 Qxc6

I watched my daughter from behind as I had before, studied her terrible beauty, attended to my terrible love. That we shared blood held little meaning for me. I didn't love her for her blood. I had fallen in love with her. I remembered the moment it happened. Sarah was three months old, and though I was happy, however scared to be a parent, my love for my daughter until that day had felt abstract, amorphous, distant. I was wiping her sour spittle from my shirt when I looked at her rather expressionless little face and I fell. Deeply. Completely. Unforgivably. Now here I was on this arid mountain, in these woods, trailing in her wake. If a bear or lion came from the brush, I would kill it with my hands to protect her. My only job in life was to keep this little animal alive, and I could not do it. Behind her there on that path, I did not consider that I wanted to be a good father, wanted to be a loving father, only that I wanted to continue being a father.

Be5 h3

There was no bear or lion on that day, though there were plenty of them. We sat and enjoyed the view of Pasadena below, Los Angeles in the distance hunkered under its brown haze. There was no distinct division between the haze and the city below, but between the haze and the blue sky above it. I imagined that up this high we were more in the blue than in the haze. We ate cheddar cheese and yellow translucent apples and drank water from our canteens.

gxh3 Rxh3

Bg3 O-O-O

I could not say that I was surprised by her castling, but the move always took me in some way to another place. That two pieces could move at once seemed like magic to me, enough so that I wished I could make a similar move in real life. What such a thing would look like I had no idea. "Very clever, Madame Nenarokov."

"Where is Mom?"

"Teaching."

"Right."

e4 e5

Outside, it looked as if it might actually rain, but we knew it wouldn't.

"What happens when you miss class like you did today?" Sarah asked.

"Sometimes I make it up, but that's hard. Usually I simply extend my office hours so the students can come see me if they want. It's only a big deal if a teacher makes a habit of not showing up."

"Oh."

"You know, sometimes people just get sick." I was sorry as soon as I said it, but nothing registered in her face.

"Grace Tilly got a smartphone," Sarah said.

"Really? What will Grace Tilly do with a smartphone?"

"Call people. Look up stuff."

"Do your other friends have phones?" I asked.

"Not yet."

"Then who is she going to call?"

"So, no smartphone."

"I'll talk to your mother."

d5 Qd6

Qa4

The most heartsickening part was that I had come to recognize the bare, vacant expression before it had fully settled on Sarah's face. This time her eyelids fluttered. Her breathing became alarmingly shallow. She convulsed once and then came back to me as quickly as she had slipped away. Seconds. Her focus became what it had been.

When Sarah was just months old, she would scare me nightly. She performed a sort of stopgap breathing that left one wondering when and if the next breath would come. I would fall out of bed and stand over her until it did, and then she would breathe on as if all was right with the world. No one ever warned us about these sounds. I felt completely unprepared to care for this creature.

"What are you thinking about?" Sarah asked.

"Excuse me?"

"It's your move."

"Oh." I studied the board. She was moving me around. I could sense the end coming. "I guess I need to move my king."

"I love you, Dad." This came from nowhere.

I looked at her face, but she was staring at the pieces in front of her. "I love you too, bug."

"Do you like baths?"

"What?"

"Baths, do you like them?"

"I suppose. Gotta get clean every now and then. Why?"

"Theresa says that baths are better than sleep."

"Better how?"

"I don't know. More restful, I guess. I told her I didn't like sleeping and she said I should take baths."

"Why don't you like sleeping?"

"I don't know."

Kb7

Rad1 Nb8

In those frightful, horrible flashes of seizure, I apperceived what it would be like to finally lose, surrender my daughter. The episodes were small destructions, and I withered alongside her each and every time. Mere seconds. Infinite seconds. I felt bad, guilty even, for feeling a perverse happiness at having witnessed the seizure alone. I wanted all of my daughter that I could get, and I wanted her selfishly. I wanted to cache moments and freeze them for parceling out over the balance of my so-called life.

Nf3 Nxe4

Qc2 f5

When I was seven, I watched my father get crushed by the weight of a failed tenure bid. I of course didn't understand what was going on at the time, but I remembered a change in his posture, how he went from saying, I thought proudly, that he was a professor at the University of Chicago to uttering, almost under his breath, that he was an adjunct professor at Roosevelt. I didn't know until years later how he had struggled to piece together a life for us, that the unfinished book on Ralph Ellison that had been a passion, that lost him tenure, was now an unfinished book that meant nothing good to him. He took other jobs on occasion, among them driving a taxi, and fell hopelessly into himself. When I was just fourteen, I was the one who found him in the basement with only most of his head intact. My mother and I were not close after that, but I never felt a sense of loss, something I always chalked up to a failure in my character. She took a job at a travel agency after my father's failed tenure bid and never seemed too happy about it. I always imagined that she left for exotic places every morning, sunny places with palm trees that somehow also failed to make her happy. I left her to join the Marines and she hated that. She died of stomach cancer gone undetected when I was in college. I held her hand while she died, and it felt strangely emotionless, I think for both of us. I was, in fact, quite sad, but she seemed so thankful for her end that I had to respect it. I had been an only child, and with her death I was completely without family. I never felt that aloneness, or at least acknowledged it, until I learned I would lose my Sarah.

I never told my daughter stories about my parents, my childhood. She was surrounded with stories, very good ones, of Meg's parents, Meg's siblings, Meg's childhood. But I never shared much, my belief being that I didn't have much to share, that I didn't remember much, which was true enough. In my mind, in my heart, I had not come into full existence until the birth of my daughter.

I had taken to working in my office late, or at least starting out there before finding myself at a near-campus tavern. I was in my office at ten one evening when Hilary Gill stopped at my open door.

"I want to thank you," she said. "Again."

"Why? You did the work."

"You know what I mean."

I nodded.

"Why are you so prickly with me?" she asked.

I was impressed with her directness. I liked it. "Am I?"

"Yes."

I didn't say anything but closed the folder on my desk.

"You don't think you are?"

"I know I am." I had a notion that she expected or wanted an apology from me. Since I had been thinking about my father, I mentioned him. "My father was an English professor. When I was a kid, I found him after he killed himself. I used to think he committed suicide because he didn't get tenure."

Hilary didn't know what to say.

"Now I know it was because he didn't satisfy himself. I found his so-called dissertation among his things after my mother died. There was no work there. He didn't receive tenure because he didn't care about the work. If he didn't care, then why would that cause him to kill himself?"

"Are you all right?" Hilary asked.

"You kill yourself because you don't live in this world." I stopped long enough to see the concern on her face. "I'm sorry, Hilary."

"What's going on?"

I stood and put things into my bag.

"Zach?" Hilary came close and put her hand on my arm. "What is it?" She put herself in front of me.

"My daughter is dying."

Rfe1 g4

It was an innocent enough hug, one meant to comfort a friend upon the discovery of shockingly sad news. I accepted the gesture, received the hug, put my arms around Hilary in response. As we pulled away, however, our faces were mere inches apart. I don't think I knew who leaned in, who initiated it, but Hilary Gill and I kissed, not much of a kiss, but a kiss nonetheless.

We stared at each other for a few seconds.

"I'm sorry," I said.

"It's okay. You're upset. I understand."

"No, really, I'm so sorry." I collected my bag and made to leave.

"Do you need to talk?" she asked. "I'm here to listen. Forget the kiss. You're upset. Let me be a friend."

I rankled at the sound of the word *kiss*. "I'm quite all right." I backed her out into the corridor. "I've got to get home."

"I'm here to talk whenever you want."

She was kind or perhaps understanding enough to not ask for any details about my daughter's condition. I appreciated that, though I was none too happy to have her present at that moment. Without saying anything else, I walked away.

Rxe4 gxf3

It is true that I can find many small flames in one fire. It being a cool night, I made a fire in the place of my house. I was poking at it when Meg came into the room and sat behind me on the ottoman.

"This was a good idea," she said. "It's been a long time since we had a fire. It's such a nice fireplace."

I nodded. "Have you looked in on Sarah?"

"She's peaceful."

"She would love this," I said. "Remember how she used to get hypnotized by fire? I'll make another for her tomorrow night."

"She'll like that."

I sat back away from the popping wood. "When did life become such bone ache?" I asked.

"Remember your idea for a furniture store?" Meg asked.

"What's that?"

"You said you wanted to open a store that sold only footstools and call it the Ottoman Empire. That was on our first date."

"And here we are," I said.

"Here we are." Meg cleared her throat, a nervous tic. "I keep waiting to wake up. This has to be a bad dream."

I pushed a log and got the fire to flame up.

"What are we going to do?"

"We have to be strong for Sarah. What else can we do? We can't let her be terrified. I couldn't take that."

"Yes."

"You know, we're going to lose her before we lose her." I hated the way that sounded, almost flippant, but I didn't mean it to be, of course.

Meg cried. I did too. But I didn't pull myself up to sit next to her and hold her. We stared at the fire and wept.

Reel f4
Qf5 Rdh8

I didn't follow Meg to bed that night. Instead I grabbed a flashlight and took a short hike up the trail. The scariest part of walking at night was before I was on the trail, fearing that I might be spotted by a cop. Still, I practiced no stealth whatsoever but instead shined my light wildly and let my boots fall heavily. Lions are nocturnal, and I wanted my presence known. I felt some relief when I found the path. I didn't want to go far up the mountain, just far enough that I felt I was in the wild, alone.

I sat on a big rock and switched off my light. It was not a wise move, but I felt compelled to do it. I was in the deep dark. The sky was clear. I stared up at the sea of stars and listened to the arroyo in front of me. I imagined that I might hear the padded steps of a cougar, but that was unlikely. It was feasible that I would hear a bear popping brush. As a stinky human I had little chance of experiencing either.

A familiar sweet smell found me. It was marijuana. Someone was in these woods getting high. I didn't mind that they were high. I did mind that they were there. I made my way back down the trail, my light off this time.

Sarah and I sat down to complete our game. I felt little hope for myself. I loved the bloodthirsty look in her eyes.

"You are a mean person."
"I know."

Rxe5 fxg3
Re6

"Ah," she said and made her move. Rxh2
I saw my predicament. I knew what I had to do. I resigned.
"It's okay, Daddy."

la grande finesse n'est pas celle qui s'aperçoit

Paris.

The best part of any flight, long or short, is being able to say that it was uneventful. Sarah slept most of the eleven hours. I was surprised by this but certain of it as I had watched her through the entire flight.

We made the long hike to passport control and found that things moved rather quickly. Sarah flirted with a little girl ahead of us in line, the zigzagging queue allowing them repeated meetings. I held our three passports. I opened Sarah's and looked at her eight-year-old face, her eyes big and dark, her hair even wilder than it was now. At the checkpoint the officer smiled and studied me, then smiled at Sarah, glanced at her passport, and asked her name.

Sarah stared at him and said nothing. The pause was excruciatingly long and awkward. She was not having a seizure, that was clear to me. She had heard the question. She could not find her name.

Meg nudged her with "Sarah?"

"Sarah," she said.

"Long flight," I said. That apparently satisfied the man.

"Are you okay?" Meg asked Sarah.

"Fine."

The officer smiled at Sarah. "Bienvenue en France."

"Merci beaucoup," Sarah said.

Out of customs and in the taxi, I felt myself fading. It was late morning, and I knew that the best thing to do would be to stay up until the evening, but I was fighting a losing battle. The freeway slowed and I closed my eyes. The rumble of the engine, the wind through the cracked open window beside me, the barely audible French voices on the radio, the fear of having watched my daughter forget her name put me to sleep.

I was awake long before we arrived at our hotel and none too happy about it. We inched through city traffic on what I was convinced was a meter-serving scenic route. That was fine as Sarah was so thoroughly enjoying the ride.

"The Louvre, Mom," she said. "Can we go there today?"

"We'll try," Meg said.

"Nous sommes mardi," the driver said. "The Louvre is closed on Tuesday."

"Are you tired, Daddy?"

"I'm fine, sweetheart."

We checked into our little hotel off the rue Saint-Placide. As I was told the rooms were quite small, I had reserved two. The rooms turned out to be next to each other with no adjoining door. With both doors closed, I felt so terribly far away from my family. I wanted to crawl onto the bed, not only because I wanted to sleep, but also because I wanted to pull the covers over my head to escape. I stepped into the corridor and gave them a knock.

Meg let me in. Sarah was lying on the twin bed nearer the window.

"Is she asleep?" I asked.

"She lay down and that was it."

I took a step and stood over her, studied her face. "She slept the whole way. You think it's just the excitement?"

"She forgot her name," Meg said.

"We don't know that," I said. "Maybe she just spaced out, wasn't paying attention." Even I didn't believe what I was saying. "I guess this is what it's going to look like."

I thought of how we take for granted that the space of the world and the time in which that space exists and in which our immediate experience is located are really the only space and time that matter. Yet somehow I believed, like all others, that moments are causally connected, tied together and moving influence in only one direction.

"Does your room smell of cigarette smoke?" Meg asked.

"A little," I said. "I can't smell it in here."

"I can." She opened the window a crack, folded her arms across her chest against the cold.

"France," I said.

Meg sat on the sill with her back to the window. "Should we wake her? I don't want her to be up all night."

I nodded. "That sounds right." I nudged Sarah. "Hey, slug, let's go out and see something."

"What time is it?" Sarah asked.

"Time to find some grub," I said. "In French that would be grubsine."

"I want a real French croissant."

"I'll bet we can find you one. Croissant or pain au chocolat?"

"Chocolate."

"I say we get cleaned up before we go out," Meg said.

"She's right," I said.

"Yeah," Sarah said. "You stink."

"I do, do I?"

"Yep."

"Okay, I'll be back in ten minutes."

"Ten minutes?" Meg said.

"Fifteen?"

"Twenty."

When traveling, I am always taken by the thought that it was just too easy to get there. I never felt that way merely crossing the continent, but there was something about crossing an ocean. The sidewalk felt just like a sidewalk at home, but it was not. It was a French sidewalk covered with French grime under French feet in French air. We walked down the block and past a few shops, around the corner, and into a patisserie we couldn't resist. The pastries were colorful and arranged as they would never be arranged back home. Sarah loved the art of it, but still all she wanted was a pain au chocolat. I watched her bite into it, eyes closed. She giggled at the explosion of crumbs and flakes, said, "Parfait." Meg smiled the way she smiled the first time we put Sarah in a swing at the playground. The child's smile and laughter were irresistible, and Meg smiled until her face hurt. She was in pain but could not stop laughing and couldn't bring herself to end Sarah's pleasure. I ached similarly. I remembered our daughter's chubby cheeks, so fat that one could see them from behind. She had grown through the air into a tall, thin girl with long feet. As she enjoyed her treat, I hoped that she could not see the sadness in me.

We walked to the Jardin du Luxembourg and through the park. I wanted to sit by the boat pond, but Sarah and Meg convinced me it was too cold.

"I wish I had a boat," I said.

"Would that make you happy, Daddy?"

"A red boat."

"I'm hungry," Meg said. "For food, not pastries."

"I know where we should eat," Sarah said. "The Café de la Mairie. It's really old fashioned. Look it up on your phone."

Meg did. "It's not far. Saint-Sulpice."

"Let's do it," I said. "Allons-y."

We chatted over an authentic and truly plain meal, complete with a waiter whose rudeness was amplified to entertain tourists. He was amusing and harmless enough. The people watching was fun, but

I was out on my feet. I believed I could make the walk back to the hotel, but I wouldn't last much longer than that. I followed along as we made our way back. At dusk the holiday lights were soft, white, beautiful. My daughter was happy.

After all that exhaustion and wanting to sleep, when I got the chance I couldn't do it. I lay in bed and watched strange talk shows, stranger variety shows, dubbed American cop shows from the nineties, but no sleep. Finally, I switched off the set and was reminded how difficult it is to not think.

Sarah had always loved paintings, and though she had not been raised with religion, she gravitated toward works with spiritual, usually Christian import. She would laugh and comment, with an irony that seemed beyond her years, "They're just like comic books. Too much to believe."

I would nod. I knew she didn't believe in a god, but what if she did? I wouldn't stand in her way. In fact, I couldn't have stood in her way. It seemed unlikely that she would ever fall for it, and I had to admit a certain relief. Still, it would have been nice to have some deity step in and do whatever it is deities do, maybe fix my daughter.

We moved through the Louvre at my daughter's pace. That day, none too fast.

Stories of Saint Jerome and the Lion, c.1425, Master of the Osservanza. The grateful lion looks nothing like a lion, perhaps why Jerry was persuaded to get so close.

The Retable of Saint Denis, c.1416, Henri Bellechose. Sarah liked the painter's name. Henry Beautiful Thing. She liked the bishop behind bars. Bishops belonged behind bars.

Watching Sarah, I was confronted with the truth of life's ephemerality, the sad impermanence of everything. These moments in Paris would not be memories she would even have a chance to look back on. She would have these joys and very soon forget them. She did not know enough of what would happen to her to appreciate how fleeting these brief experiences were. Yet somehow, maybe on a cellular level, she must have understood, as she made her way so slowly from painting to painting. When moments are weighted, the most insignificant details become meaningful. So it was then, each painting marking a place in her story.

Meg and I were still, quite visibly, feeling the effects of jet lag. Why Sarah wasn't, we had no idea. It was a kid thing.

"I've got a bad case of museum legs," Meg said. "These marble floors are sucking the life out of me."

"Me too."

"She's taking forever. Can you hurry her up somehow?"

"I wouldn't if I could. She's loving it."

"She is, isn't she?" Meg sat on a bench and looked up at me. "Have you noticed anything today?"

I shook my head. I felt bad for being possibly unobservant, a sin in this moment in our lives that was unforgivable, for being so tense. How could I enjoy my daughter when so tightly wound?

"Think we can pull her away for a quick snack?"

I studied the back of Sarah's head; the mop of uncontrollable brown hair made her head look like a balloon set atop a stick. "Hey, slug," I said. "Want to go downstairs and grab a bite of something? Mom and I are a little hungry."

"Okay," she said.

"That was easy," Meg said.

"Ask and ye shall receive."

The Rolin Madonna, c.1435, Jan van Eyck. There is Mary all dressed in red instead of being mantled in the blue of heaven. The sullen baby Jesus is in her lap. He is unwilling to play patty-cake with the grim donor.

For some reason, and when I say some I of course mean unknown, as we walked south along rue de Rennes, I regarded Meg and could not help but be critical. I was finding fault, and I didn't want to. I thought back to when Sarah was two and was having what some called behavioral trouble, a lot of screaming and recalcitrance, what I called spunk, and remembered Meg yelling at the child. She was at her wits' end, I knew that, but her impatience, her noise led to more noise. She would scream and the child would scream louder. One night I said something that was true enough, but it bothered me for a couple of years. Without much consideration I said, "If you can't control yourself, why should she?" Meg fell silent, her feelings hurt much as mine would have been. At the moment of my utterance, I had been clear and certain about what I had wanted to communicate, but once I said it, I felt nothing but stinging regret. The ironic and finally sad benefit to me was that Sarah drifted closer to me. In those moments when she needed quieting down from her night terrors, I was the one who sat with her, holding her, making soothing sounds. She now was plenty close to her mother and affectionate enough with her, but even Meg noted how much softer the child was with me. It was something that hurt her feelings. Right then, during that walk, all I could focus on was Meg's yelling.

"Daddy, can we go back to the Louvre tomorrow?"

"If that's what you want. I thought we might try the Eiffel Tower."

"Louvre," she said.

"You got it."

"Which painting did you like best today?" Meg asked.

Sarah thought about it.

"Let me guess," I said. "It was the one with the baby Jesus in it."

"They all have the baby Jesus," she laughed.

"That's one mean-looking baby, that's all I have to say."

"Not in all of them," she said.

"I guess not. But in plenty of them. Dour baby."

"Mary doesn't look much happier," Meg said.

"That's because she's got that mean baby," I said. "Why do you like those paintings anyway?"

"I told you. Because they're so weird."

"I'll bet nobody ever told that baby what to do. How do you tell a god to eat his peas? Stop playing with your food, Lord."

"Don't pee in the tub, God," Sarah said.

"You two are going to hell," Meg said.

"When?" asked Sarah.

We walked on awhile in silence.

"We should swing past Le Bon Marché and look at the Christmas decorations in the windows," Meg said.

"Sounds good," I said.

Lady with Pansies, c.1475. Ophelia would say some hundred years later, "Pansies are for thoughts." Pensées. Pansies. Perhaps the first French pun I understood. She wears a ring on her thumb.

"Daddy, can we go back to the Louvre tomorrow?"

I looked at Meg. I could see her moving toward tears.

"Of course, honey. That's a good idea. The Louvre again tomorrow."

The Pietà of Villeneuve-lès-Avignon, c.1455, Enguerrand Quarton. The ashen Mary watches and Mary Magdalene weeps, listens to the plucking of thorns from Jesus's head by John. Sarah thought that John was removing his halo.

When your child is dying, it is damn near impossible to think about anything else, to enter into distracted conversation, to enjoy a meal or a piece of music or a book. I tried to find glimpses of joy or peace or whatever word fits as I watched my daughter navigate her last chapter in ignorance of her condition. Why tell her? I thought this and felt weak for doing so. Why, since she would, even if she did apprehend it all, fade into dementia and not remember anyway? Why scare her now? Why take these moments of joy or peace or whatever word fits away from her?

The sky had taken on a greenish twilight that looked more appropriate for a coastal town, and so I imagined that it might rain. Instead, it began to snow, a light flurry.

"Isn't it wonderful, Mommy?" Sarah said.

"Yes, it is," Meg said.

For some reason Sarah's calling Meg "Mommy" instead of "Mom" struck me. It was not unusual for her to say that, but it drove home the fact of her youth. I was grief and sadness walking, but I could not let myself sink into a pit. I had to be strong for my child. I had to be strong for Meg. Still, while thinking such a noble thought, I wondered how I might continue without my daughter. If I could have died for her, as if sitting for an exam in her stead, I would have done so in a heartbeat. And I knew Meg would have as well. I tried to take some solace in the fact that Sarah was well loved and that she felt that, was feeling that in life.

"What if we just walked forever?" I said.

Sarah turned to look at me.

"What if we never went back to our hotel or back home?" I stepped forward to hold her hand. "What if we simply walked and walked forever?"

"To the horizon," Sarah said. "That would be perfect."

The snow fell a little harder.

The display windows of the fancy department store, Le Bon Marché, were well worth the modest detour. They were elaborate and understated at once, each a work unto itself. A few required patience as they unfolded gradually, while others were mere explosions of color and motion. At another time, in another universe, the spectacle might have been almost enough to make me like Christmas. Meg wanted to make one. Sarah wanted to live in one. I wanted my bed.

The Ship of Fools, c.1500, Hieronymous Bosch. Oh, our proclivity for neglecting the immortal soul. Bad nun. Bad monk.

Meg and Sarah wanted to walk through the store, and so we did. I had to admit that somehow the merchandise here appeared superior to any of that I recalled from the stores at home. It did not take long to re-alize, however, that it was all in the presentation, the arrangement of colors, the way things were given space. How exactly it was pulled off I had no idea, but I came to see that all the clothes were exactly what I would find at home, the same styles, the same materials, the same brands. Somehow a plain Woolrich field jacket looked rugged and ex-otic folded and stacked on the table of Le Bon Marché. Magic. In short order, however, I had had enough. As our hotel was only a couple of blocks down the street, I told them that I would meet them back there.

The snow now seemed significant, as if it might amount to something. It was falling in huge flakes now that bothered my face, lingered for seconds on my coat before melting away. The tempera-ture had fallen enough that I actually felt cold, not such an un-welcome feeling; I liked the novelty of it, being from Los Angeles. I also appreciated that the sensation distracted me ever so margin-ally from other concerns.

I collected my key at the desk and walked up the four flights to my room. I peered out the window at the eddy of people in the snow. The cars, seemingly all black, were backed up single file along the rue. I watched out for Meg and Sarah. I didn't want to lie down because I knew I'd fall immediately to sleep. Though not hungry, I wanted to dine with my family. At that moment, I wanted to see my daughter walking up the street toward me, just to observe her familiar gait, merely to see her approaching my position in space in present, living, promising motion.

My room was dark behind me.

I was leaning out into the cold air when I spotted the two of them. I waved as they crossed the intersection, but they didn't see me.

From the other end of the block I heard a Christmas song played on trumpets. The sounds of the horns bounced off the buildings, and in spite of the music itself, I enjoyed the playing. I looked to see the two men with horns. They paused beneath windows, and people tossed coins down into a hat one of them held. They stopped beneath me and looked up. I dropped a coin to them, and that's when Sarah saw me. She was thrilled by the sight of me hanging out the window, the music, the snow. She moved like she was about to become a teenager but looked like a child. I could see this on her face so easily. What I could also see easily was the look of stress on Meg's face.

The Knight, the Young Girl, and Death, no date, Hans Baldung Grien. The skull bites the dress, a foot in a boot placed against a rock for leverage. Its bone lies separate, severed, isolated near the hooves.

After dinner in a bistro at the end of the block, we returned to the hotel for the night. Meg did not report to me what had happened in the department store. She did knock on my door and place a damp pair of panties in my hand.

"Thank you?" I said.

"Those are your daughter's."

"That's creepy. They're damp."

"Yes, they are."

"Where's Sarah?"

"She's in the shower." She took back the underwear. "She leaked."

It was all happening so fast, or at least things seemed to be; that it was happening at all made it too fast. To leak a little urine was such a small loss of motor control. To repeat oneself was something I did every day, often several times. But each small thing was magnified, amplified for us—mere whispers were shouts; tiny flickers were blinding flashes. It was quite likely that we were also missing some symptoms altogether.

There was something there in the dark. I could imagine it in there, rustling in the dry leaves, dragging itself, perhaps. The sun was beating down on my back, burning my neck. I was always lax about using sunscreen, a disregard that came with dark skin, but I knew I was burning. Yet I could not tear myself away from the mouth of the cave. Members of my team were far off, uninterested in me or what I had found, doing something at the river's edge. How a breeze was able to blow from within the cave I did not know, but it smelled of leaves I knew but could not identify. Ordinary things became puzzles; I felt this happening. The opening of the cavity was quite clearly what it was, and yet it made no sense to me. Confused by the breeze, I found the mouth of the cave to be something else altogether. There was a monster here, and that mouth was its mouth, that face of rock was its face, that wind was its breath.

"Why do you stand there like a thief?" the monster asked me.

"I am no such thing," I said, startled by a diction that was not my own.

"What do you want from me?"

"What do I want from you?" I looked around. "You are the monster. I want nothing from you except that you go away."

"Where would I go?" the monster asked. "This is my place. This is where I have been and will be. Give me back my bones."

"What?"

"Give me back my bones."

I didn't get away from the cave, and so I turned to connect the ropes beside me to my sling so I could rappel down to the river's edge. But the breath of the monster turned me back to it.

"Take what you want," the monster said.

I lit a match in the bright daylight, thinking it would help me see better. When it flared to life, the day became dark, and all I could see was the flame. I heard the movement again, the rustling.

My father called to me from below. I couldn't see him, but I knew his voice well enough. "What a terrible thing, to watch a child die," he called.

"It is," I called back.

"Is there nothing you can do?" he asked.

"Nothing."

"Perhaps," he said. "Perhaps."

I awoke only to wonder if I was still asleep. I knew that my daughter's bed was just on the other side of the wall behind me. I put my hand to it and imagined that I could feel her heart beating.

What is it you want? the monster had asked. What do you want? the monster asked.

I lay awake for the balance of the night letting my dream shatter into indecipherable pieces the way dreams do. I would reconstruct it later in ways that made little if any sense, ways that would yield a vague belief in some meaning that I desired. Dreams were not important; it was the reconstruction of dreams that was always significant. Therein one could find a window, a clue or a vein, longing, fear, and guilt. I didn't know what my reconstruction of that dream sought to tell me or what I sought to create in remaking it, but it troubled me perhaps beyond reason.

We were at the Louvre the next morning, and Sarah resumed just where she had left off, viewing paintings that bored me silly, the religious significance of which mattered little if at all to her, but it was clear that she enjoyed them honestly and, strangely, without irony. I was told by the concierge in the hotel that the best way to enter the museum was through the metro stop below. And so we were able to avoid the long queue, which meant I was not nearly as exhausted or irritable as I had been the day before.

"Tell me again what you like about this room," I said.

Sarah looked around, sighed, and gave me the best of all possible answers. "The colors," she said.

I made a complete turn, looked at every wall. She was, as ever, right. If I looked at nothing but the colors, I found the room near perfect. It was nothing but reds from rose to ruby, crimson, brick, blues from phthalo to cerulean, cobalt. A sadness came over me.

My daughter would continue to teach me even as I was losing her, and yet there was so little I could offer her. My job had been to prepare her for life. Now, with what was coming, it made no sense to even consider preparing her for death.

The Head of John the Baptist, 1507, Andreas de Solario. Sarah loved the painting and I hated it. "The shaft of the platter looks so much like a skinny human neck," she said. "Like he's really not dead at all."

We exited the museum through the pyramid on the mall. Our plan was to meet Meg at the Jardin des Tuileries for lunch. It was cold and there was snow around the bases of trees and on what grass was there. It was crowded, more crowded than I had imagined it would be. I worried briefly that we would be unable to find Meg. I smelled ground coffee beans and caramel and wondered why the two were mixed. The odor served to make me hungrier. Sarah was nearly skipping. She had had that little bout of incontinence, if that was what it was, and a couple of forgetful moments, but there had been no seizures that we had noticed.

"I don't see your mother," I said.

Sarah scanned with me. "Are we early?"

"A few minutes," I said. "Want to have a hot chocolate while we wait?"

"Chocolat chaud, oui," she said.

I waited through a short queue and then sat on a bench and blew on our drinks. "Très chaud."

"Muy très chaud," Sarah said.

We laughed at that.

"I take it we're lucky to see snow here," I said. "Apparently it's been rare the past few years."

"I liked it last night."

"Yes, it was pretty."

"Daddy?"

"Yes?"

Sarah sipped her cocoa.

"You have a question?"

"No, it's nothing."

We stared off into the same space.

"There she is," Sarah said.

"Where?"

"Over by the trampolines. She doesn't see us."

"She will, just sit tight. Enjoy your chocolate. It's good, isn't it?"

Meg did finally see us. She waved and walked toward us. She was carrying a small paper sack and her purse. She decided to take a shortcut through some bushes. Stepping through the snow, she could not see the brick or rock that tripped her. She fell but not all the way down, catching herself against a small tree. I trotted the eight or ten yards to her, leaving Sarah on the bench.

"I'm okay," Meg said.

"Good. We're just having some hot chocolate."

Meg looked past me to wave to Sarah. "Zach?"

"Yes?" I turned to see that Sarah was not on the bench. We turned in circles looking for her. I saw the heads of the children on the trampolines going up and down. I looked for her wild head of hair.

"Where is she?" Meg asked.

"She was on the bench," I said. "Sarah!"

Meg called her name as well. Passersby looked at us.

"She cannot have gone far," I said. "You go that way toward the fountain. I'll look back the way of the museum."

"Zach?"

"I'll meet you at the fountain." I called her back. "You say, 'Je cherche une fille brune. Elle porte un manteau rouge.'"

She repeated the words back to me.

I did my best not to panic. Though the air was chill, I was colder inside, icy. I looked at every face, short or tall. I imagined it would be easy to spot my child because there were so few brown faces, but

I did not see her, and so that thought steered me again toward dread and panic. I found myself trotting and worrying while I moved whether I was going so quickly that I might miss her. Soon I was out of breath, leaning over with my hands on my knees, still looking everywhere.

A young woman walked quickly toward me and stooped to pick up something from the ground. "Excusez moi, monsieur," she said.

I thought she might know something about Sarah, so I attended to what she was trying to tell me.

"Vous avez laissé votre bague ici."

"What?"

Then, in English, "You have dropped your ring."

I recognized the scam right away, though I felt stupid for letting her get even that far. "Go away," I said.

"This is your ring," she said. She tried to hand it to me.

"Non!" I used my hand to shoo her away. "Je ne suis pas intéressé." She didn't just move away from me, she ran.

I looked to my left to find that a policeman had stopped next to me. He asked me if I needed help without opening his mouth, just the tilt of his head.

"Ma fille. Elle a douze ans et est brune. Elle porte un manteau rouge." I held my hand in the air to indicate her height.

He studied me, nodded, tilted his head as if to tolerate my poor French. "Don't worry, we will find her," he said in English. Somehow his French accent was reassuring. He spoke into his radio.

"My wife is waiting by the fountain. Maybe she's found her."

"Where is the last place you saw her?" he asked.

I pointed. "A bench over there."

"What is her name?"

"Sarah. Sarah Wells. She might be a little disoriented. She has a medical condition and can have seizures." I felt as if I were somehow betraying my daughter by offering that information.

The policeman reported that information into his radio. He looked at me. "She is black? Like you?"

"Oui."

The policeman and I walked to the bench and continued on toward the fountain. I searched every face, not only to see if it belonged to my daughter, but also searching for any suggestion of knowledge of her, as if there might be a conspiracy. My mind was racing. I felt my hands shaking and I tried to stop them.

"I too have a daughter," the policeman said. He was looking too, his head moving in sharp microturns, snaps of several degrees at a time. I wondered if that was a real way to search or if he had been taught that in gendarme school, a method to give panicked parents confidence in his efforts. "She is younger than your daughter."

Another policeman fell into stride with us.

I spotted Meg, hugging herself, turning circles near the fountain. Sarah was not with her. She saw us approaching and stopped turning, shook her head. "There is my wife," I said.

The new policeman peeled away from us and headed past the fountain toward la place de la Concorde

"Where did she go?" Meg asked. She sounded angry.

"It's all my fucking fault," I said. "I shouldn't have walked away from her." I had turned away for only a second, but why even that?

The policeman received a call on his radio, then looked at us. "No, it was something else."

"Could someone have taken her?" Meg asked.

"She probably just wandered off and became lost in the crowd," the policeman said. "It is easy to do."

I thought of the river and grew more afraid. "We should go over and check the Seine," I said.

We walked that way. That was when I saw the rear side of a long rectangular building. I paused and observed the low hedge surrounding it. "What is this building?" I asked.

"This is the Musée de l'Orangerie," the policeman said. "Impressionist paintings are in there. Monet's *Water Lilies*."

"Can we look in there?" I asked.

Meg looked at the building, then at me, and nodded. It apparently made sense to her that Sarah would wander into a museum.

I was convinced, hopeful, that we would find Sarah sitting on a bench in front of a Cézanne or a Matisse, and she despised Matisse, and that that would be the end of it. Neither the two old women at the reception desk nor the security guard had seen a girl matching Sarah's description, but they invited us in to look. The tense walk through the giant oval halls of the Water Lilies searching for my child was surreal; the light was surreal, and so, I suppose to distract myself, I observed that irony of that surreality against the huge impressionistic murals. A swing through the rooms yielded no daughter, no evidence that she or anyone like her had been there.

Meg was too far into shock to cry, but I might have been. The fact was, I was angry, perhaps at myself, I didn't know. The anger manifested in my snapping at the nice young policeman.

"So, what are you people doing?" I asked. "Our child is lost out here somewhere. What are you doing? Where are the other policemen?"

"We will find her," he said.

"You keep saying that."

Meg took my hand. More as an expression of fear than to calm me down, though her touch had that effect.

The Wedding Feast at Cana, 1563, Pado Caliari. "It's so big," Sarah remarked about the canvas. Parked beside me on the bench in front of it, she was staring, she told me, at the dogs in the foreground and the cerulean of the sky behind. The halo looked fake, as, of course, it was.

We crossed the busy street on our way to the river. I couldn't imagine my Sarah alone in the middle of that traffic. On the other side we walked down the stone stairs to the wide path along the Seine. The sight of the dark water caused my breathing to catch in my chest or throat, my mouth. I realized that my fear was keeping me from searching. I began to try to study the faces along the bank, but I couldn't resist looking at the river.

"What are you looking at?" Meg asked me.

"I don't know." I didn't know why I was thinking I would see Sarah in the water, but I thought just that.

The policeman's radio crackled. He stepped away, listened, talked, came back. "We have found your daughter."

"Thank God," Meg said.

"Where is she?" I asked.

"Near where you saw her last," he said. "I will take you back there."

"Thank you," Meg said.

We climbed the stairs back up to street level and found the lane filled with protesters carrying signs and chanting. "Dieu dit non!" they shouted. "Dieu dit non!"

"God says no?" I asked the policeman.

"They are against men marrying men," he said.

I did not consider any opinions about the crowd's cause, but I hated that they were making it difficult for us to cross the avenue. We wanted to get to our child and they were in our way. I grew angry and came near shouting at the marchers.

"I can't believe this," Meg said.

"Dieu dit non!"

We wended our way through the mass of people, their faces a mixture of ugly anger and glee. I found ways to hate them all, for their politics, for their noise, for their nastiness, for their simply being in my way. One woman who looked like she had stepped right out of a painting of the French countryside appeared to snarl at me. We made it to the other side of the road and walked past the impressionist museum and discovered a flurry of police activity, police shouting, police trotting, police pointing, police pushing nonpolicemen behind things, all with policely concern. Our policeman was talking into his radio and was now visibly agitated. He stopped us with a half-raised arm.

"What is it?" I asked.

"What's wrong?" from Meg.

I pushed past our policeman and stepped around the tall hedge. Almost immediately I spotted Sarah. She was some forty yards away from me across the bare-ground plaza. It was what was between us that was causing the fuss. A white man held a pistol high over his head and was shouting at the top of lungs, "La voix du peuple, l'esprit de la France! Renvoyez-les! Renvoyez-les!"

Sarah cowered behind the sturdy leg of a big policeman who stood with his automatic rifle at the ready. She was terrified of course. She found my face across the commotion and pleaded for my help. The man with the pistol continued to shout, even louder now, and wave his weapon. He turned his blond head and looked in the direction of my daughter. I don't know what came over me, but I became convinced that this right-wing fanatic was zeroing in on the dark skin of my child. He was turned away from me, and all of a sudden I was sprinting toward him. He turned to me just as I was on him. I collided with him hard enough to knock him over. I grabbed the pistol, twisted it, and bent it back against the outside of his hand. I thought I heard his finger break, and I thought even then that I couldn't have in that din. He didn't let go. The police were on top of the two of us immediately. They were as rough with me as they were with him. I was elbowed in the back of the head and had my arm wrenched behind my back. I saw Meg running to Sarah. Sarah screamed for me; her voice sliced through the shouting of men. The policemen asked me again and again what I thought I was doing. I didn't understand the French, but the tone made the meaning clear. The word *bête* was repeated. Sarah and Meg managed to get to me. I was handcuffed. I dropped to a knee to let Sarah wrap her arms around my neck. A policeman pulled her away. The cop who had been helping us explained to the others what was going on, then he looked at me and asked in English what I thought I was doing.

"I'm sorry. I was afraid for my daughter," I said in English. It was too much of an effort to find the words in French.

"That was stupid," he said.

"I know," I said.

Meg looked at me, held my face, and stared at me like I was crazy.

"I'm okay," I told her. "I don't know what I was thinking. I saw him looking at Sarah." I was pulled back to standing by a policeman. "I'm okay."

Meg did not look like she believed me.

"Daddy?" Sarah said as I was pulled away a few steps.

The handcuffs were removed, and I stood there rubbing my wrists while they asked me questions. My mouth and throat were dry, scratchy. What was my name? What kind of name was that? Did I know the man with the gun? Had I ever seen the man before? Where was I from? Did I have military training? Did I have a history of mental illness? Why was I in the country? When would I be leaving?

Somewhat satisfied, they let me go.

Gabrielle d'Estrées and One of Her Sisters, 1594. Pinch, pinch. My daughter laughed, returned to it again and again, laughed at it again and again. Pinch, pinch.

The wisest know nothing.

Als sei kein Unglück die Nacht gescheh'n

The more I thought about what I had done in Paris, the more my action confused and upset me. To say that I hadn't been thinking clearly was of course an understatement. It was more accurate to say that I had not thought at all, even with so much on my mind. But just what did that mean? To not think. I guess I was simply my animal self, not that an animal would have been so stupid. Something went through my mind, however rushed. Uncensored, certainly. Ill considered, obviously. My action at any other time might have caused major problems between Meg and me, but, given all else, the matter fell away.

Weeks passed. Christmas Day came and went. An annoyance, as always, but poignant this time, as the activity of counting Christmases occurred to me. The morning of gift opening was sweet enough, boring enough, sad enough. The same was true with the coming of the new year. And then the new semester began, distinctly marking time as they always did. Semesters came and went so quickly, so innocuously, that they felt like nothing until they were counted, and then the sum was decades. I never saw *old* coming.

Episodes of forgetfulness or spaciness were noted now and again. The seizures did not worsen; however, they occurred more frequently. We observed usually two a day, if in fact that was what they were. The fear of course was that there were others that we did not witness. For that reason, both consciously and un, we hardly ever left our daughter alone. This neither went unnoticed nor was it liked by the twelve-year-old. I imagined how I would have felt if my parents had loomed over me every second of every day, and so I managed to force myself to give her some space.

School began again for Sarah, and that presented new problems. We couldn't keep her home, and though I didn't want to tell her teachers, it was necessary. They had to not only be on the lookout for seizures and changes in them, but they also needed to understand that there might be a difference in her work and attention. I hated the teachers' reactions. Pity and premature condolences.

Ms. Boone, Sarah's sixth-grade teacher, was straight out of central casting. She was perfectly postured with her hair done up in a bun. She nodded a lot.

Meg briefly described Sarah's disease.

"Oh my," Ms. Boone said. "What can I do to help?"

"Just watch her," I said. "She might space out from time to time, but we don't even know if that's a symptom. She might be merely daydreaming."

"But we need to know if she's doing it more frequently," Meg said.

Ms. Boone made a note on the paper in front of her.

"Things are going to get a lot worse," I said. "Sarah will have to leave school. We don't know when that will be."

From the look on Ms. Boone's face, I could see that the gravity of the situation was becoming apparent.

"Sarah is going to die," I said. It felt strange stating it so bluntly, at once terrifying and, in a sick-making way, freeing.

Ms. Boone put down her pencil. "Oh my."

Later that night, Meg and I sat in front of the idle fireplace. "Did you see the look on Ms. Boone's face?" Meg asked.

"The *oh my* look," I said. "We'd better get used to it."

"Why?" Meg started to cry.

I pulled her close. There was nothing to say. There was nothing to do.

In my dream I was back on the streets of Paris, not far from Notre-Dame, on the left bank, near the English bookstore Shakespeare & Co. I wore a yellow slicker, the kind with a reflective silver stripe, even though there was no rain. I stood outside an Orange mobile phone store. The store was packed with customers, unhappy customers. They had all taken numbers and were all visibly displeased. Just outside the door, sitting on the sidewalk, back against the wall, was a Roma woman. She held a spotted puppy, perhaps the cutest puppy I had ever seen. The open box she had put beside her for money was empty. The puppy hardly moved in her arms. She looked at her empty box and then at me. She sighed, stood, and walked away. I followed her. I was just five or so paces behind her, and either she was remarkably oblivious or completely indifferent to my presence because she did not once turn to eye me, suspiciously or otherwise. I followed her through the busy 6e and into the Jardin du Luxembourg, where she sat next to another woman dressed as she was, who could have been her twin or her. She handed over the puppy. The second woman, the new woman, shot me a hard glance that, frankly, more scared than startled me. I followed her anyway, followed the puppy, recalled in my dream how in movies everyone says to follow the money. I followed her the long walk to Montparnasse. The woman sat on the cold ground outside the station and positioned the docile puppy on her lap, wrapped her shawl around it. Then it was no longer a puppy, no longer a dog, but a child, a little child. Girl or boy I could not tell, but it was docile like the puppy had been. There was no puppy now, only the woman and the child. She put her open box beside her and put a few of her own euros into it. Still, no one else dropped any money into her box. I walked up to her. I emptied my pockets of all the money I had. It filled the box. The woman stared at me. I could not see the child's face. I wondered if it had a puppy's face.

"I wish I had more to give," I said.

"Je m'en fou!" she shouted. "Je m'en fou!"

Gewoben vom verblendenden Geschicke

Hilary Gill had made it through the departmental vote regarding her tenure, no small feat given her lack of work; but the quality of her work and the promise of it had persuaded most of us. The harsh news, and harsher because the news came so quickly, was that the dean had denied Hilary tenure. The response within our ranks was not one of surprise, and there was not much desire to push back. Not even I was surprised. However, I became immediately irate, first because the decision had come so quickly as to appear an insult to our judgment and second because I was constitutionally disposed to find the actions of any dean or upper administrator suspect, ill considered, and wrong.

I walked into Hilary's windowless office and sat on the hard chair beside her desk. We sat there without speaking for a minute or so. I looked at a picture on the wall that I imagined was her sister, but I didn't ask. Hilary sighed, got up and shut her door, came back to sit at her desk.

"I'm sorry," I said.

"It's not your fault."

"I'm afraid I got your hopes up."

"It felt good for a while," she said. "Being hopeful."

"You realize that this is complete bullshit. The dean knows shit, that's the first thing. If the department says yes, she should say yes."

"Well, she didn't. I appreciate your support. Believe me."

"I can't let it go."

She laughed. "What does that mean? Listen, I didn't do the work. You told me that a long time ago."

"You actually did do the work. You just didn't happen to show it to anyone. Well, until now."

"Anyway."

I stood, perhaps a bit suddenly. I was angry.

"What?"

"I'm going over to talk to that asshole," I said.

"The dean?"

"Yes, the asshole dean. Do you know another asshole I need to talk to?"

"Don't do that," Hilary said. Hilary stood and put her hand on my arm. "I don't want you to talk to the dean."

"The chair should do it," I said.

"We talked about this before. I told you, I'm simply not cut out for academia. It's not my thing."

"First of all, that's bullshit. You're a good scientist. You're a great teacher."

She shrugged.

"Let me talk to the chair."

"No." She kissed me gently on the lips.

I kissed her back, then pulled away. "I'm sorry," I told her.

"About what?"

"I never should have kissed you."

"I know that," she said.

"I'm sorry."

"It's okay."

"I've got a lot on my mind these days." I knew I sounded nervous, scared even. I was suddenly thinking of Sarah. I sat down again. "I'm confused about a lot of things in my life, and I'm afraid I was sort of using you as a distraction."

"I see."

"I don't think you do," I said. "I'm really sorry."

"I hear you." Her voice was even, almost monotone.

I felt my shoulders sag.

"Are you okay?" She put a tentative hand on my shoulder. I heard her swallow. "I didn't mean to upset you."

"You didn't upset me," I told her. I reached up and tapped her hand. It struck me that Hilary was understandably, rightfully distraught, but that her concern for me was somehow odd. "Listen, if you don't want me to talk to anyone, I won't." I stood. "Well, I've got to go try to teach these people something." I looked for the window that was not present in Hilary's office. I wanted to kiss her because I knew it was the wrong thing to do, a feeling or thought that made no sense at all to me but made all the sense in the world. I was not attracted to Hilary at all, did not want at all to be close to her, to be intimate with her, to know her any better than I did. Yet, I wanted to kiss her. Had I not needed to leave for class, I don't know what I might have done or why. "We can't do this anymore," I told her. I walked to the door.

"Can we get together and talk later?" she asked.

"I don't think so," I said.

"I'm sorry about everything," she said.

I didn't understand her apology. I stood frozen for a beat. "You're certain you don't want me to talk to the chair?"

"Yes. It's too late for that anyway."

I had gone into Hilary's office to offer help, perhaps comfort, but I ended up being the one comforted and finally offering her some extra pain. I was not happy with myself, needless to say. I was, in fact, ashamed. But like so much lately, I had no idea how I had so deftly stumbled into the muck. I went on to class and delivered my lecture on autopilot. I had the sinking and sobering feeling throughout that it was one of my better performances; it seemed I was so much better when I was not fully present.

The plain package contained the plain shirt I'd ordered in a larger size. Tucked discreetly under the collar was a neatly rolled yellow Post-it square with tiny writing. It read, "Por favor ayudenos. No nos dejan ir." *They will not let us go.* Outside my den window, I could see clouds gathering against the hills.

In diesem Wetter, in diesem Braus

After picking up Sarah from school, I took her for a short hike in the hills. It was unusually cool, especially as we gained some altitude. However, the sky was cloudless, cerulean, and brilliant. It was that bright California light that I often found harsh and disliked. We spotted a few birds, but then Sarah seemed to grow listless. She began to space out more and more and then suffered one of her seizures, one that lasted somewhat longer than any we had observed. Needless to say, our walk down took considerably longer than the trek uphill. I had not taken my phone with me, and so we returned to the house to find a worried mother. She became more so when she saw my expression.

During dinner Sarah was actually chatty, uncharacteristic for her recent self. She told us about some girls who were visiting her campus from some other local school. She reported that two of them had gotten into a rather nasty fistfight.

"They were such apes, these girls," Sarah said.

"What was the fight about?" Meg asked.

"I don't know. Clementine Gilbert said it was all about a boy. But I don't know. Both of them got sent home. I didn't really see the fight, but I could sure hear it. They sounded like cats. I saw one of the girls after. Very tall with red hair and freckles. Clear marks of a hooligan."

We laughed. It felt good to laugh a little. It served mainly to underscore how quiet we as a family had become.

Sarah tired. She became quiet, and we could see a weakness in her eyes. We put her to bed.

In the kitchen, I washed the pots and pans while Meg nursed a mug of tea. The mug was one that was once broken, and the handle had been glued back on. She insisted on using it whenever she saw it.

"I didn't think the deterioration would be so fast," she said.

"I don't know if it actually is fast. I mean, we don't have anything to compare it to, after all."

Meg nodded. "Seems fast."

It was my turn to nod. The house felt too quiet, too still. None of us had laughed in our old way, the way we had tonight, for far too long. We seldom played music in the house, and yet music seemed missing. I felt as if I was dying inside, but I didn't say that. Even thinking it seemed so selfish as to make me uneasy. I felt an anger toward Meg that I knew was misplaced and unfair, and, recognizing it as such, I was able not to act on it, but not shed it. I wondered if she felt anything similar.

"I want to talk to Dr. Gurewich and ask her when we should expect what," Meg said. She set her mug heavily down but held on to the handle.

"That sounds right." The question we really wanted to ask was how long we could expect to recognize our daughter.

A scream found its way to us from Sarah's room. Meg and I stared stupidly at each other for several seconds before running. When we arrived at the child's bedside, she was asleep, as peaceful as if nothing had happened. Perhaps nothing had happened. Perhaps everything had happened.

That evening, Meg and I undressed, bathed, and went to bed at the same time. It had been such a long while since that had happened. For as long as I could remember, she or I found work or some other reason to stay up well after the other. Lately, it had been mostly me. On several occasions I was not even at home when she went to bed. Though tonight I felt a need to hold her, or to be held by her, and sensed clearly that she too had the same need, we did not come together but lay there in the darkness, facing the ceiling. I listened to Meg's breathing change as she moved into sleep. She always pushed a tiny stream of air out of a small aperture between her lips with a little pop with each exhalation. There were times when she would feign sleep, but I always knew. Though I never knew why she would feign sleep. I would fight sleep tonight, as I did most nights. I was afraid of dreaming. Perhaps not so much afraid as uninterested.

Ein Lämplein verlosch in meinem Zelt

Nothing appeared different as I bought my coffee in the shop behind the library. The little round lady at the register asked me, as she always did, whether I wanted a muffin or croissant with that. Students studied their phones. I walked into the department office to check my mail. Tim, the office manager, looked at me with a blank expression I had never seen on his face.

"What is it?" I asked.

"Hilary Gill," he said.

"Yes?"

His eyes were wet. He was just this side of crying. He looked out the door and down the corridor, then back at me. "She committed suicide last night."

"Excuse me?"

He didn't repeat his words. He didn't need to. I heard him the first time. Had he repeated himself, those words I would not have heard. He readied himself to tell me more, to give me details.

I raised my hand and stopped him.

I walked away toward my office but passed it by, then passed Hilary Gill's office as well. I did not look at her door.

All the things that people think when they learn of a suicide passed through my mind. Mostly I wondered if she had been telling me the last time we spoke. Worse, I wondered if she had been asking for help. Sad in so many ways, that I had been too tone deaf to hear her message or her plea, and that, even if I had understood her, no one was more incapable than I was to offer comfort or help.

Und den Kopf ich drehe

coda

Man hat sie hinaus getragen

Why do people speak of things coming full circle? If a thing does not come *full* circle, then there is no circle at all. It is like *past* history or a *hot* water heater or *end* results. Things do not traverse a *full* circle of meaning so that we discover their proximity to their opposites.

Across the long and very old Stanton Street Bridge from El Paso, Texas, is a not-so-little town in Mexico called Ciudad Juárez. Friendship Bridge, Puento Rio Bravo, Puente Ciudad Juárez-Stanton El Paso. Hundreds of women had been hunted there, on the other side of that bridge, pursued, raped, imprisoned, tortured, and killed. They were mostly dark haired and of slender build, as was my beautiful Sarah.

Time slipped away. Cliché, yes. True, yes. Days, months, life not marked by clock or calendar but by the decline of my daughter's health. The seizures became more severe, far more frequent. Sarah would forget where she was going, what she was doing. Her friends fell away quickly; they were children. That was just as well, as their

135

names were more and more often a mystery to her. She had not yet misplaced her mother or me in her memory, but it was coming. She would sit for hours just staring. We hired a nurse to sit beside her and stare into space with her. The stress of it all, the sadness of it all, the inevitability of it all drove a fat wedge between Meg and me. She withdrew into manic exercise, yoga and cycling. I failed at burying myself in work but succeeded at staring for long periods at the return address of the packages that had delivered the handwritten notes pleading for help.

PO Box 219
Bingham, NM 87832

I would go there.

And then there was a day when my daughter wandered from the house when no one was looking. We were always looking, but for one brief moment we each thought the other was looking, and so no one was looking and out of the house stepped our child. We searched the house over and again, then the street and the next street. Neighbors we did not know searched their yards. Meg talked to the police while I drove around. Then I thought of our trail, her talk of lions and bears, her big feet one at a time raising dust, and I went there. It was just dusk of a day that had been far too sunny, far too warm for the season. I hiked up the mountain, keeping in mind at every bend that if she had gone this way, there was no reason to believe that she would have remained on the path, and so I looked for signs, for footprints that the hard, dry surface would yield only grudgingly. Up the mountain looking for large scat that I hoped to not find, scanning the far ridges for the flash of a white tail tip, listening for rustling or perhaps even singing, as it was our habit to sing in these woods that supported bears and cats. I worried that my daughter might be running through these woods and so appeal to a cat's instinct to chase. I imagined that she might be experiencing

her first period and so lighting up the air with a pheromone entice-
ment to a wayward bear. I distracted myself by remembering that
bear in French was *ours* and imagined that the bear might then be
ours. I paused every several hurried steps to listen, to stare ahead
at the trail and to the sides for anything broken, for any transfer of
soil onto plant matter on the ground. Then I heard a whistle, or at
least an attempt at a whistle. I listened hard. Again. I slid down off
the trail toward the sound and there she was, sitting on part of a
downed tree. I worried that there might be a snake that she had not
seen, and then I felt stupid and neglectful for not having worried
about her encountering snakes during my climb.

"Sarah?"

She turned and stared at me. She did not know who I was in
that moment. I died some. I died quite a bit. I sat beside her, looked
around for danger.

"This is a nice spot," I said.

She said nothing. She was not having a seizure, but she said nothing. She played with the cuticles of her thumbs.

"Let's go home." I reached over and took her hand, and I saw a
flash of recognition in her face. I looked at my mobile phone and
saw that I had no signal. We walked together. We sang. Lydia, oh
Lydia . . .

Here comes an old soldier
from Botany Bay

a pocketknife

The way we treat each other changes at a pace that in all other are-
nas of human experience we would find intolerable. We might call
the pace slow or unhurried or, most accurately, glacial. A glacier is
a body of ice and firn that shows evidence of movement, occurring
where the production of snow is greater than ablation and so con-
tinues from year to year, persisting even when a change in climate
reverses the conditions that have allowed it to exist. So it is with the
indecency, harm, and evil we inflict on each other, prejudice, ne-
glect, torture, and slavery. Like glaciers, they are not unique to any
one part of Earth. Like ice, it is both mineral and rock.

In case you forgot, my name is Zach Wells. It would not be so
strange or awfully bad if you had forgotten. After all, my dear
daughter will forget me, my face, my voice. It is inevitable. That
means I cannot stop it from happening. It means that no one can
stop it from happening. I suppose God could, but of course It has

better things to do, bombs to drop, tornadoes to wind up, disease to unleash. There finally is also the fact that, well, there is no God. But there is a devil.

As my daughter moved ever closer to losing her voice, what young voice she had managed to attain in her brief and beautiful life, beautiful until life became what life becomes, my voice too changed, as inevitably, as necessarily. Logic is a harsh master. However, another quite undeveloped voice remained constant, stabile, even resolute. That voice had no timbre, no volume, no depth, no resonance, was a voice scratched out across small paper in blue ink, an unwavering plea for aid.

The postman will not tell you who belongs to what mailbox in the post office. I knew that, and so I didn't bother wandering into the tiny Bingham, New Mexico, post office to ask the question. I could not hang out in the post office waiting to see who opened the box of interest. It was a one-room affair. I therefore mailed a big red-paper-covered box to PO Box 219, Bingham, NM, 87832. Then I waited hour after hour after hour, day after day after day, three days in my Jeep, pretending to look at topographical maps and aerial photographs on my dash, three days in the diner across the road, pretending to study maps and photographs on the table in front of me. I told anyone who wondered about me that I was a petroleum geologist and that I believed there was oil in the area. I left my perches when the postman left for lunch. When the postman left at five, I drove to the little town of San Antonio at the junction of the I-5 and US 380 and slept in a Motel 6, with air-conditioning and cable TV.

On day one I sat in one of the three window booths of the Bingham Eatery. They had just months earlier had the seats and stools re-upholstered with new vinyl that did not quite match the very old Formica veneer of the tables and counter. The vinyl still smelled new. The clashing reds were unsettling to my eyes, but I was comforted to discover that I was not alone, as the first thing the waitress, DeLois from her name tag, said to me was "Sorry about the colors, but it hasn't really made anybody sick yet."

"What brings you here?" was the second thing she said. She was a middle-aged, stout, blond woman set atop spindly stockinged legs. She actually wore a uniform, light blue, a deliberate relief perhaps from the fighting reds.

"Work," I said.

"It would have to be, 'cause we ain't on the way to no place. There's no passing through Bingham. You're either here because of whatever weird shit brought you here or you're lost. I pegged you for lost."

"I'm plenty lost," I said, "but I know where I am."

"What kind of work?"

"I'm a geologist. I'm looking for oil."

"I ain't never heard of oil in New Mexico," she said. She tugged at the sash around her middle, her apron. It dented her.

"Not yet," I said.

"What will you have?" she asked.

I looked at the menu, black marker on whiteboard, set high on the wall behind the counter. "The griddle cakes?"

She gave a surreptitious sidelong glance back at the window to the kitchen and offered me the faintest shake of her head.

"Oatmeal?"

DeLois stared at me without moving.

"Huevos rancheros?"

She nodded, then called the order back to the cook.

"Your name is interesting," I said.

"My parents couldn't decide on Delores or Lois. That's the story they told me, anyway. Actually, I don't think they could spell worth a damn and this is what I ended up with. School is a good thing."

"I'm Zach."

a pocketknife, a tarp

For whatever reason, the tiny post office that served the few people of Bingham opened at seven thirty in the morning. It was barely light. The restaurant didn't open until eight, and so I felt not only conspicuous but suspicious sitting in my Jeep. I spread out maps of the central New Mexico region but worked on my own data from my cave in the Canyon, so my time wasn't being completely wasted. When the cook and DeLois drove in and parked behind the diner, I went inside and had breakfast. DeLois made small talk with me. I learned that the cook's name was Jorge, though he wanted to be called George. At lunchtime I drove west to San Antonio and sat briefly in my motel room before making the long drive back to the parking lot of the post office, where I sat in my vehicle until it closed at three. That afternoon I toured the dry, desolate, monotonous countryside and wondered just what the hell I was doing way out there in the middle of no place. That night I called Meg and asked after Sarah.

"She was quiet today," Meg said. "Where are you?"

"I need some time. I'm working."

"Are you in the Canyon?"

"I will be soon. There's a cave here in New Mexico that I'm checking out." I hated lying. "Does she even realize that I'm not there?"

There was a long pause. "I can't say that she does." It scared Meg to say it. She was not concerned about my feelings but about what it meant about Sarah.

"There will be days like that," I said. "I'll be home soon. I'm sorry I've run off."

"I'd like to run off too, you know."

"When I get back."

"That's not what I meant."

"I'm sorry."

We hung up and I lay back and stared up at the crumbling ceiling. I watched a documentary about bears and fell asleep in my clothes.

Morning three. While I ate my too-hard-scrambled eggs and sausage patties served on a blue plastic plate, I peered through the booth window and saw the red-paper-wrapped package I had mailed from Socorro two days earlier exit the post office. It was carried by a white man with a shock of white hair, of medium build, wearing desert khaki camouflage pants and shirt. He was accompanied by a taller, fatter man, similarly dressed. The second man carried a stack of boxes that he loaded into the back of a Hummer. He then returned to the post office. The first man tore through the red paper and into the box, discovered it empty. When his friend came back with another stack of packages, they had an animated conversation that concluded with the shorter man kicking the box and red paper around the gravel parking area. They got into their huge rig and rolled away to the east.

I pulled my pages together, left a generous tip, and walked out to my Jeep. I drove east behind them. I saw only a couple of vehicles on the road, most parked off the highway at shabby or even derelict collections of structures. There was enough traffic that my presence was in no way conspicuous or suspicious. Well ahead was the Hummer, easy to spot on this landscape. I saw it turn north toward uneven terrain. I could see from the highway as I passed that the Hummer came to a stop at a chain-link-fence-surrounded compound with a large warehouse and a smaller building. There was an old school bus parked there as well, the rust as prominent as the yellow against the white landscape. It was also easy to see that there was virtually no way for me to approach the compound without becoming immediately and unfortunately conspicuous and suspicious.

I noted where I was by the mile marker, drove east another mile, and then turned around and headed back to San Antonio.

That night I called home and received a report on my daughter's deterioration. It was apparently going well. Irony and humor were something I understood to be a human way of handling tragedy, but I wondered if it was to be experienced alone, whether it was normal to find the funny in misery without an audience. I decided it didn't matter.

The two men, Shock of White Hair and the big guy, walked toward the diner, leaving their Hummer parked beside the post office.

"Oh Lord," DeLois said.

"What is it?" I asked.

"These boys give me the heebie-jeebies." She looked at me as if for the first time. "Stay away from them."

The men eyed my Jeep as they approached, like dogs noticing something out of place. When they entered, they made more noise than a mere two men should have. They sounded like they were coming in from a terrible blizzard, but there was no storm, snow, rain, or otherwise, even without the stomping of their tan canvas boots. They gave me a sidelong and none-too-friendly glance as they took seats at the counter. I couldn't hear the questions I saw them putting to DeLois, but she gave me a nervous look that might have been a suggestion for me to leave. I went back to my maps, or at least pretended to go back to my maps. I now knew who was sending me the clothes I had ordered, but I didn't know who was sending me the written messages. One thing was clear: it was neither of these two men.

DeLois came over and topped off my coffee, left me without saying a word, but her apology hung in the air.

The shorter of the men cleared his throat loudly, swiveled on his stool, got up, and walked over to my booth.

"How you doing?" he asked.

"Fine. Kind of you to ask."

He looked back at his heavy partner, then gave me a quizzical look, a half smile. "You're not from around here."

I resisted the obvious sarcasm, opted for "No, I'm not." I looked him in the eye. "My name is Wells."

Another look back at the counter.

"Jeff," he said.

"Pleased to meet you." I did not offer to shake his hand. The sleight went unregarded.

"Why are you here?"

"Breakfast."

"Wells," he said. "What are you doing in Bingham?"

"Looking for oil."

He thought I was joking at first, was about to complain to me or his pal, then looked at my maps. "Oil," he said. "Here in New Mexico?"

"I'm looking. I'm a geologist."

"Who do you work for?"

"I'm not allowed to tell you that," I said.

"You're not, eh?"

"Part of my contract. My employers would rather not have people know they're looking into the ground. I'm sure you can understand that." My heart was racing.

Jeff signaled for his buddy to come join us. They sat across from me in the booth. They looked slightly comical, all fatigued up like that. Still, they scared me, and I was fairly certain they could see that.

"Wells, this is Roger."

I nodded.

"Wells here is looking for oil," Jeff said. He pulled a cigarette from a pack and put it between his lips. "Here in New Mexico, if you can believe that." He lit the cigarette, blew smoke up toward the ceiling.

"No smoking," DeLois said from behind the counter.

Jeff paid her no attention.

"Oil," Roger said, as if to prove he could speak.

"Why do you think there's oil around here?" Jeff asked.

"Some surface features from satellite images," I said.

"Where?" Roger asked.

I said nothing, finished my coffee. "I'm looking at a lot of places. Groundwork takes a lot of time."

"There ain't no oil in New Mexico," Jeff said.

"There *ain't* no *discovered* oil in New Mexico."

"So, how's it going?"

I smiled and pulled together my maps.

Jeff stopped me. "Where looks good?"

I had a brief staring competition with him, then folded. I pointed to a spot on the map, their compound. "Around here from the satellite imagery, but I need to check the area out. Right behind the post office over there looked interesting at first but not anymore."

"Right here?" Jeff asked, his dirty index nail tapping the map.

"Yes."

Jeff looked at Roger. Roger looked at the map. It took the big man a while to realize what Jeff was telling him.

"There's an alluvial field there, and that makes it hard to read the surface. So much washing away of the sediment." I was talking out of my ass, more or less. "Since there are no extant fields here, I can read the biostratigraphy of the sites. It just seems to me that, given the oil in similar zones in Texas, there should be similar productive capability here." I looked at their glazed-over eyes. "Sorry to bore you with this."

"How does it work?" Jeff asked.

"What?"

"Suppose someone found oil on my land—would it be mine?"

I laughed. "Hell no. You might own the land, but you don't own what's under it. A company that finds it has the right to come in and take it."

"What the fuck?" Roger said.

"What if we found it?" Jeff asked.

"If you found it on your land and managed to take it out, then it would be yours to sell. Same with gas."

"So, if some company found it, I wouldn't get nothing?"

"You would get a lot," I told him. "The oil company would have to pay you to be on your land, to move across your place to get to the product. There are formulae for figuring the payments."

"How do you find the oil?" Jeff asked.

"I went to school for eight years to learn that," I said. "If I tell you, then what good am I? I'm just saying."

Jeff nodded.

"I'd better get to work." I put money down for DeLois. "Gentlemen." They did not detect the irony.

a pocketknife, a tarp, a map, a compass

I was supposed to be a petroleum geologist looking for oil out in the desert, so I went out into the desert and looked for oil. I pretended to search for oil. I parked myself on a desolate spot within fairly easy eyeshot of the camouflage brothers' compound. The tarbush and acacia weren't thick enough to offer shade even if they had been taller. I had come with some diagnostic instruments from my department at the university. Some core-sampling tools and an electronic sniffer. I didn't know how to operate the sniffer and had my doubts, as did many others, about whether the thing actually worked at all. None of that mattered, of course. I would not have been able to find oil if I was standing knee-deep in it. A light drizzle fell, and I looked up to see some clouds clumping together in the southwest. The compound was quiet. The Hummer was there, parked by the bus, but I didn't see anybody moving around. Then, as I was about to leave, I saw a woman walk, slump shouldered, from the house to the warehouse. I thought a lot about my daughter while out here too, about how much I missed her, about how insane it was that I was out here in the middle of no place up to God knew what. I thought about work, about how the importance of it had faded through the years. What did I ever think I would learn or discover? Did I ever believe it mattered? And I thought about Hilary Gill. I imagined that one might see her work through to publication. That was what *one* might do.

I watched as a dually pickup arrived. The men unloaded boxes and big bags and took them into the warehouse. Nothing seemed terribly heavy, and it was clear that they were laughing and joking the whole time.

I packed up, wondering as I did it if I was technically *pretending* to pack up. I drove down the hill and stopped at the northern fence of the compound, got out, and paced the ground there. The window-less (at least on my side) warehouse was not as large as I had thought, a hundred feet long at best and perhaps half as wide. The corrugated roof and sides were in need of repair and paint. I felt so terribly lonely out there, so lonely that feeling began to fascinate me.

I heard an engine, not big like the Hummer's or what the bus must have contained, a two-stroke perhaps. When I looked up, I saw a three-wheeled ATV coming toward me on the other side of the fence. It was Jeff and his white hair. Behind him I saw Roger and another man standing outside the door of the house.

"Oh, it's you," Jeff said. He was wearing a sidearm.

"Yeah, it's me," I said. "Jeff, right?"

"Finding anything?"

I shrugged. "This your place?"

"Yep."

"Just inside the fence?"

"Why?"

"Just asking."

"Where are you staying? You camped out someplace?"

I didn't answer. "Frankly, you guys scare me. The camo, the gun. The way you looked at me in the diner."

"We're harmless," he said, not sounding at all harmless. "So, you finding anything out here?"

"Would you mind if I took some readings inside your fence? Around that wash." I pointed to the drainage. The deep rut ran a jagged course parallel to the big building.

"You can do that." He paused, looked back at the house. "If you find something, you tell me first, right? This is my property, so you tell me before the oil company, right?"

I sighed as if making a decision. "If I find anything promising, I will be sure to tell you first."

"Gate's over here."

Two men I hadn't seen before rolled open the gate while Jeff watched. He didn't introduce them to me but climbed into the passenger seat of my Jeep.

"I'll ride with you," he said.

"You don't want your trike?"

He laughed, not a real laugh.

"What kind of business you got here?" I asked as we drove past the warehouse.

"Storage."

"No trucks?"

"They're all out." He didn't like the questions. "So, what looks so promising over here?" He pointed to the hills and finally to his own land.

I stopped the vehicle and we got out. I walked to the wash and he followed. I bent down and picked up a couple of rocks, tossed one away, and handed the other to him. "That's a diatom," I said. "A microfossil."

He examined the rock. I was hoping his hobby was not rock collecting or that he didn't have an interest in gems.

"Microfossils are the skeletons of tiny plants and animals from when this was an ocean. They are strewn throughout the layers. They give me an idea of the rock layers. I need to search around and catalog all the different kinds I can find. I'll also be using some other equipment to measure soil density and trace presence of hydrocarbon."

"Okay."

"It's boring," I said. "It's tedious."

"That's what you spent all those years in school for?" he said.

"I don't like it when you put it that way," I said. "So, it's okay if I set up?"

"Knock yourself out."

a pocketknife, a tarp, a map, a compass, a shovel

As I had in the hills, I set myself up as if to take readings, make notes, survey. What I actually did was read an airport science-fiction novel, go through my own work, think about my daughter, and drink water. I did this until I had to urinate. It was then that I made my way to the warehouse. They had given up watching me, so I looked for a door. My heart was racing. I ignored the instinct and desire to look about to see if I was being observed. My story was I needed a toilet. I found a door, grabbed the knob, turned it. It was unlocked. I walked inside. There were perhaps twelve or fifteen women opening boxes, folding clothes, packing boxes. Only one of the women looked at or cared to look my way. She gave me a double take, perhaps because she hadn't seen my face before or perhaps because my face was brown like hers. She looked away suddenly just as I felt a hand on my shoulder. I turned to find Roger.

"Whatcha doin'?" he asked. He sounded like a cartoon character.

"Looking for a john," I said, casually.

"Ain't no bathroom in here. Why didn't you just pee outside?"

"Who said I had to pee?"

He laughed. Poop jokes always make kids laugh. "Come on," he said, and he led me out of the warehouse and toward the house. He pointed to a couple of portable toilets set beside the house. "Take your pick."

"Great, thanks."

Jeff was stepping out of the house as I was stepping into the john.

"He needed to take a dump," Roger said. "He didn't see nothing."

Once the door to the awful-smelling booth was closed, I couldn't hear anything else. I sat in there long enough to be believable. When I exited, Jeff was waiting.

"So, what do you think?" he asked.

"This is awkward," I said. "What if I told you I think there's oil? Then you'd start drilling and it would all be yours. Where would that leave my employers? Or me, for that matter?"

"What if I just wanted to drill a hole in my land for the fun of it?"

"That would cost you a lot of money and time, and you'd have to know how to do it. You could probably discover some igneous rocks at two thousand feet in your test drill, but what would that tell you? This is not just a business, it's science. It's not like looking for gold in a creek."

"What if I hired you?"

"You don't even know me. I don't know you. I'm getting paid now."

"You said you'd let me know first." He was getting angry.

"I did, didn't I." I looked across the landscape. I couldn't imagine a place more desolate. "Okay, I will. I need to run these numbers. You have to remember that all I'll be telling you is whether there's a possibility that there is oil down there."

"I get it."

"And if I tell you there is a possibility, you plan to look for it yourself?"

"Maybe."

"Then where would that leave me?"

"I'll pay you."

I left there that afternoon seeming unhappy. My armpits stank from sweating through my lies. I didn't know what I was doing. If they figured me out, I was pretty sure they would kill me. The image of those women in the warehouse was stuck in my head.

I drove back to my motel room, called home, watched CNN, and took a hot bath in the insanely small tub.

In the notebook I left in the wash on the compound:

> Regarding previous ventures in the area: Section A is primarily a dip slope of the Sierra Blanca–Jicarilla Mountains. It is not as structurally deformed as the other two test sites. It consists of eleven of the twenty test drillings that were performed in the considered area. Six of the tests in Section A are spread in an east-west orientation to allow reasonable deductions about the area.

*Four tests penetrated igneous rocks in the Permian sedi-
mentary rocks. Also, four of ten tests penetrated probable
Precambrian rocks, indicating the sedimentary stratum is
at least 1,500 feet thick and at maximum 2,425 feet.*

*From surface observations of the early unproductive sites
compared to my observations of two of the sites I have examined, it is my belief that one of them is likely to yield.
Though the sniffer offered nothing promising, I am deeply
impressed by the microfossils uncovered by modest digging.*

I lay back in the tub and imagined Jeff and his cohort reading that
page. I resolved that I would not return there the next day.

But I did drive to Bingham for breakfast. I wanted to talk to DeLois.
She was pleased to see me. It was early, and she sat in the booth across
from me.

"I was afraid you would come back," she said.

"Takes more than a couple of neo-Nazis to scare me away."

She raised her eyebrows. "They scare me plenty."

"What do you know about them?" I asked.

"They were here when I got here. That was five years ago. There's
a bunch of them. I think they live together, but I don't know. They
must work in one of the quarries or mines. There ain't no other jobs
worth having."

"How did you end up here?" I asked, hoping that it didn't sound
like a judgment. If she did hear it that way, she didn't let on.

"A man."

I nodded.

"I grew up in Socorro. My father was military and for some reason figured this would be a good place to retire."

"And the man?"

"Him? Jackass. He was fifteen years older than me. He was a
manager at one of the gold mines. Sounds great, doesn't it? Even

the assholes who owned the mine were poor. Anyway, it was the same old story. He went to buy a goddamn pack of cigarettes and never came back."

"I'm sorry."

DeLois laughed. "No biggie. It took me four months before I realized he was missing."

"And this bunch of guys?"

"Why are you so interested in them?"

I shrugged. "Just curious."

"I figure they're survivalists or some shit. They often have guns in the racks, but that's not so strange around here. Ain't nothing to hunt though. Weird thing. They got these girls that they drive by in a bus, an old school bus, maybe once a week. Off to Socorro or San Antonio, I'm guessing. They never bring them in here."

"The county cops ever check them out?"

"A trooper rolls through here once in a while. Nobody cares what anybody does out here. Tell the truth, I wouldn't be surprised if they got themselves a meth lab up in the hills someplace. What about you?"

"I don't have a meth lab," I said.

She laughed. "What are you doing here? There's no oil around here."

"There might be."

She gave me a look. "Do you have a family?"

"A wife."

"No kids?"

"A daughter. I used to have a daughter." I said it not only because I didn't want to talk about Sarah but also because I was trying to adapt to a world without her.

"I'm sorry."

"What about you? Kids?"

"Thank God I didn't have any with that bastard. Too late now." She looked at me for a while without talking. "You be safe."

"Excuse me?"

"I don't know what's going on, but you be careful. Those boys are bad news. They scare me to death, and they ought to scare you too."

"Oh, they do. I'll be careful, DeLois."

a pocketknife, a tarp, a map, a compass, a shovel, a canteen

I had told an unknown person in a strange roadside diner that I would take care of myself, and it struck me, quite heavily, that I had not shown the same courtesy to my patient wife. I had left Meg to deal and cope with the saddest of all possible situations, and I would have been hard pressed—no, simply unable—to tell her why. I did not know why myself, and yet I did, quite obviously. I wished that all that I was involving myself in was merely a game, and I double wished that my daughter was again herself and playing the game with me, plotting moves as one would on a giant sixty-four square board. I considered my love for Sarah, and it brought me to consider my love for my wife. Life, and especially recent life, had pressed a wedge between us. I still felt my love for her, and at this significant distance, coming to terms, as I was, with the loss of our child, I refused to resign to the belief our love was lost. I would later write her a long and gentle, explaining letter. Dark ink on white paper. Ink on folded paper was always better than an email, perhaps better than a voice on a phone or in person. The scratching of strange symbols on leaves, marks that could be just as easily meaningless as much as they could offer meaning, like the mysterious microfossils that I had touted as geologic clues to deep and covered history and future fortune.

May was about to turn into June. The middays became hotter, but mornings and evenings remained bearable, even cool when the clouds rolled in to deliver thunderstorms. That was usually in the afternoon, but a day of solid rain kept me close to my motel room one day. My only excursion out was to the little grocery market a mile and a half down the freeway. I went there for bread, cold cuts, fruit, and any kind of cookie. As I pulled off the exit and glanced at the small parking lot, I saw a school bus. There was a man leaning against the bus, looking like he was waiting, on his cell phone having a not terribly animated conversation. He might have been one of the men I had seen at the compound. I parked and he paid made me no attention. Inside the store I walked through the produce section. I did recognize a man from the compound, a skinny fellow who had been by the door of the house. I walked past him. He might have noticed me, but if he did, he didn't care. He was busy watching several women who were shopping. They were brown skinned and would have blended into the environment had they all not been dressed in polo shirts and khaki pants. I walked to the far side of the store and browsed the cheese section. I was very near two of the women.

In a soft voice, I said, "Estoy aquí para ayudar."

They looked at me and hurried themselves along.

I approached another couple of the women. I felt like a sex offender in training. The skinny man couldn't see me now, and I said the words again.

One of the women turned and stared at me. She was frightened.

"Lo siento," I said.

She said nothing still, but she also did not run away. She looked up the aisle toward the front of the store, then back at me.

I took the first note from my pocket, held it on my open palm for her to see. "Did you send me this?" I asked.

She looked like she might scream. I held my hand away from me to calm her. I turned to leave, not wanting to scare her any more than I had.

"Espera," she whispered.

I turned back to face her. That was when the skinny man's voice scratched down the aisle. "Hey, hurry it up, chicas." The way he said *chicas* made the word sound harsh and insulting.

"Rosalita Gonzalez," she said softly, then, "Ciudad Juárez."

"Come on," the skinny man shouted.

The woman turned immediately and moved toward the checkout. The woman with her whispered something I could not hear, but the women to whom I had spoken shushed her quite clearly. I hurried through my shopping with hope of falling into line at the register behind her. When I got there, however, they were through and being herded onto the bus.

I watched them drive away as I paid for my food.

"Fifteen fifty-three," the cashier said.

I gave him a twenty. "That was an odd sight," I said.

"What?"

"All those women dressed like that."

He shrugged, handed me the bills, and the coin change slid out of a machine next to me. "They come in here every Sunday. Some kind of religious group, I guess."

"The men with them look pretty rough," I said.

"I guess," the man said. I looked at his tattoos, and it occurred to me that he didn't look so different from the compound men.

"I just meant they didn't look like churchgoers."

He stared at me rather blankly. He might have nodded. Regardless, I was left feeling awkward and anxious.

I made my way north to the state police station at the southern edge on Socorro. It was on a frontage road along the freeway and looked very much like a hardware store. The office was manned by two officers, both white, both alarmingly similar in affect to Jeff and Roger.

"What can we do you for?" the mustachioed one asked me. He was seated, but he was very wide.

"I'm not certain," I said. I was afraid to speak, not because I feared they were involved or sympathetic to the Nazis I had met, but because my story simply sounded so crazy. The notes hidden in clothes ordered on eBay, a paleontologist masquerading as a petroleum geologist camped out and spying on their neighbors to expose their slavery ring. Being here was a bad idea. My silence attracted the attention of the second cop.

"Sir?"

"I was wondering how long it will take to get to El Paso from here."

They exchanged glances.

The mustache said, "About three hours."

"Anything else?"

"Sir, what's your name?"

"Thank you," I said.

"Excuse me." The mustache stayed after me. "Maybe I should just write down your name."

"No, thanks." I walked out. I was certain one or both were watching me.

The mustache followed me out of the building and watched as I got into my car. I didn't like his posture, the way he seemed to lean toward me. I didn't like his voice. He scared me, and I didn't like that.

Halfway to my car, the sky opened completely and drenched me. I sat behind the wheel and listened to the rain pounding on the roof. "Ciudad Juárez" she had said in the market. What was she trying to tell me? I knew that the town was just across the border from El Paso, and I knew now that it was just a three-hour drive down the interstate. Without knowing what I was looking for, I headed south.

a pocketknife, a tarp, a map, a compass, a shovel, a canteen, a poncho

I drove across the bridge into Mexico, from a slightly large American town to a large Mexican city. I pulled off to the side of the road and sat. I always felt, or at least imagined that I felt, some kind of sensation when I was on foreign soil, perhaps a kind of exhilaration, maybe the promise of something novel. I could not deny that I felt that as I sat there, but it was short lived. Rosalita Gonzalez. How many women named Rosalita Gonzalez must there have been in Mexico, in Ciudad Juárez? I had no idea what I was looking for or even why. Hell, I didn't even know what I had been doing in New Mexico for the past almost two weeks. I knew that I was being a coward by staying away from my home.

A cop pulled up behind me, got out, and approached my window. "Hello, señor," he said. "Do you need some help?" he asked in fair English.

"No, officer. I'm just thinking."

"I'm afraid you will have to think somewhere else. This is a high-traffic area. You are a traffic hazard here."

"Can you tell me how to get to the police station?" I asked.

"Do you have a problem?"

"No, I just need the police station."

"Do you want the city police, the state police, or the federales?"

I had not thought the matter through. "The federales, I guess."

He gave me directions. It was not close. "Park in a lot," he said.

"Okay."

"If you park on the street for too long, a cop very much like me will take the license plate off your car."

I looked at him.

"Americans like to ignore parking tickets and just drive home."

"Parking lot. Thanks."

"Are you okay, señor?"

I nodded. "Thanks."

I drove the route suggested to me, my country to my left, within sight almost all the way, until the road veered right and away from the Rio Grande. Another left turn and I was at the headquarters of the federal police. I took the advice given and paid a quarter to park in a lot. The building was not nondescript, but there was nothing distinguishing about it and hardly worth describing. Inside there was less of a bustle than I had expected. There was no counter but a desk behind which sat a small woman in street clothes.

"May I help you?" the woman asked in English.

I felt strangely insulted that I was so clearly American. "I'd like to speak to someone about a missing person," I said.

She looked at me suspiciously, picked up a pen. "Who is the missing person? And where did you lose her?"

"I didn't lose anybody," I said.

She questioned me without speaking.

"I think I found someone." I looked beyond her at a wide flight of stairs. The uniformed men walking by paid me no attention at all, conspicuously so. "Who should I talk to about that, about having found someone? I'm not certain that she's missing, but I think she is. Could I just talk to someone?" I was talking too much, and I could tell that my English was becoming difficult for her to track.

"Have a seat over there, please," she said in a rehearsed way. She pointed at several wooden chairs lined against a wall. No one else was seated. "I will see if I can find you someone."

In short order I was joined in the line of chairs by two men, who seemed to be together, and a woman with a young child, a boy or a girl, I couldn't tell. After a good thirty, perhaps forty minutes, I was about to revisit the woman at the desk when a tall, angular man made eye contact with me as he descended the stairs. He wore a dark blue shirt with a large six-pointed star sewn over his heart. I noticed that his black boots were extremely shiny at the bottom of his dark blue trousers. I stood as he approached.

"I am Lieutenant Deocampo."

"Zach Wells." I shook his hand.

"What can I help you with?"

"I'm not sure," I said.

"I was told you believe you have found someone. May I ask what you mean by that?" He looked at his watch.

"Is there someplace we can sit down?"

He didn't sigh, but he might as well have. "Come with me."

I followed him up the stairs and along a busy corridor to a small rectangular room that was not his office. It might have been an interrogation room, but it seemed somehow too friendly, and there was a window.

"Please sit down, Mr. Wells."

I did, looked through the window at the clear sky.

Deocampo sat beside me. "Yes, Mr. Wells?"

"I understand that a lot of women have disappeared here."

"This is true. It is a sad reality."

"I met a woman the other day. She said her name was Rosalita Gonzalez. I suppose that is a very common name."

"Very common."

"I have this notion that she might be missing."

"Why do you think that?" he asked.

"I met this woman in a store in New Mexico. She told me her name and mentioned Ciudad Juárez."

"That is hardly a reason to think she is missing."

"I believe she is being held against her will."

"You met her in a market?"

"She was being watched."

"I see. Why didn't you go to the police in New Mexico? I am a policeman in Mexico. I have no power in the United States."

"Of course." I felt stupid. I had no idea why I was sitting in that room with him. I blew out a breath and pressed on. "Perhaps you can tell me, is there a Rosalita Gonzalez who has been reported missing?"

Deocampo stared at me for a long few seconds. He walked across the room to a small table on which sat a very old computer. He worked there for a few minutes, then stopped and studied the screen silently.

"Rosalita Gonzalez was reported missing three years ago. She was twenty-three at the time."

I didn't say anything.

"Do you know how many Rosalita Gonzalezes there are in Mexico and the United States?"

"A lot," I said.

"How old was this woman?" Deocampo asked.

"It was hard to tell," I said. "She could have been twenty-one or forty."

"I am a policeman in Mexico, Mr. Wells."

"I know."

"Three hundred and six," he said.

"Excuse me?"

"Three hundred and six. That's how many women have been killed or gone missing, most of them killed."

I nodded.

"I cannot help you. Go home."

a pocketknife, a tarp, a map, a compass, a shovel, a canteen, a poncho, a trail

I wanted to go home, in fact. But I told him, "I need to know. This person asked me to help her."

"She did?"

"Yes." I looked at the man's eyes and realized how weary mine must have appeared. "Is there a photograph of the woman?"

His shoulders sagged as he leaned into the back of his chair. "What do you do for a living, Mr. Wells?"

"I'm a university professor. I'm a paleontologist."

Deocampo raised his brows.

"I study fossils." Language was getting in the way. "Dinosaurios."

"Really? My son loves them."

I nodded.

"Do you have any children, Mr. Wells?"

"I have a daughter."

"You should go home to her."

"Someone needs help," I said.

"You really believe this woman is a prisoner," he said more to himself than to me. "Come with me."

Lieutenant Deocampo led me out of the conference room, down the wide stairs where I came in, along a wide hallway lined with portraits of uniformed men, to a narrower corridor, and then down a straight flight of stairs. He opened a heavy but unsecured door and waved his arm for me to enter before him. Inside the large room were crates upon crates, stacked boxes, and an entire wall of file cabinets, floor to chin high, all set against walls painted the sort of pale green found in old hospitals.

"This is what three hundred and six dead and missing women look like," he said.

I said nothing. There was nothing to say.

He dragged his finger along the faces of the file cabinets as he walked. "Here we are," he said. He slid open the drawer second from the top and found the green folder he wanted, opened it, and held it for me to see. "Rosalita Gonzalez," he said.

I studied the picture. It was old, frayed at the bottom. It showed a woman standing in front of a small house with an older woman. The young woman held a small dog in her arms, a Pekingese, maybe.

"Is this the woman you saw?"

"I can't say," I said, reaching out and touching the picture with the tip of my right index finger. I traced the outline of her face, touched the dog. "I saw her only once, and this photo isn't very clear."

Deocampo closed the folder. "You seem like a good man," he said. "There is a lot of sadness here because of this. It is easy to get people's hope up. Is that how you say it?"

I nodded. Hope, hopes, it was the same thing. I saw no need to correct him on such a small thing, or even a bigger thing.

"Maybe the police in New Mexico will listen to you?"

As he said this, I wondered why I had not gone to the New Mexico police at first. Perhaps it was because I saw them as white, but, frankly, they scared me, seemed too much like the men I was reporting. More likely it was because I didn't have a real story to tell them.

"There are others," I said. "I think some white men are holding them as prisoners. Slaves."

Deocampo put the folder back into the cabinet and pushed in the drawer. He paused his hand on the handle.

"I don't think the police in America will believe me. I think my story sounds crazy. It does, doesn't it?"

"Not so crazy. You believe you saw a missing woman. It happens every day. Here, a woman goes missing every day."

"What should I do?" I asked.

"Where do you live?"

"Los Angeles."

He looked at me, I thought, as if that piece of information helped him better make sense of all of this and me. "Go home, Mr. Wells. Be with your daughter."

"You're not going to call anyone, are you?"

Deocampo looked at his watch. "How much time do you have? Do you have time for a drive? An hour?"

"Of course."

Some said that three hundred young women had been killed or disappeared in some twenty years. Others said it was closer to seven hundred gone. People are like that about numbers. They will say it is not seven hundred but only three, two hundred, as if one hundred would not be truly horrible, fifty, twenty-five. No one knew who killed and kidnapped these people. Maybe drug cartels, some said. Maybe roving gangs of sexual predators. Devil worshippers. Perhaps invaders from space. Men. It was men. It was always men. Always men.

The numbers were so very large, obscene, fescennine. Olga Perez. Hundreds of women have no name. Edith Longoria. Hundreds of women have no face. Guadalupe de la Rosa. Names. Name. Maria Najera. It was so uncomplicated, safe, simple to talk about numbers in El Paso, a world away. Nobody misses five hundred people. Nobody misses one hundred people. In Juárez, it was one. One daughter. One friend. One face. One name. Somebody misses one person. Maybe Rosalita Gonzalez.

Deocampo's car was royal blue, late eighties, a Buick sedan, as clean as the day it rolled off the assembly line. Even the floor mats were pristine. I hated putting my big boots on them. He could see my stiffness.

"Do not worry," he said. "I will clean the mats. I clean them every week."

"I can see that."

"My wife likes a clean car. And a clean house. And a clean husband."

The ride took us back along the river the way I had come. The afternoon had become hot and uncomfortable, but the lieutenant appeared unfazed in his buttoned-up shirt and tie. He turned left and we gained some elevation as we rolled into an industrial area that had seen busier times. He stopped the car and we got out. I followed him past a loading dock of some long-defunct business into a yard of discarded metal and mounds of baked hard earth. We stood above a subdivision of modest homes, mostly one-story affairs with postage-stamp lawns. Across the river were the high-rise buildings of El Paso.

"This is where we found the bodies of eight women," Deocampo said. He kicked at the dirt with his shiny shoes. "This is the reality we deal with every day. I don't know if my phone is going to ring and I'll have to go out and find a body. Families come in every week with stories and photos. I don't have time to check out the leads I get here, much less think about things across the border. There was a head right where your foot is."

I looked down and stepped aside.

He looked over at the reasonably safe city of El Paso. It looked like Oz.

"What could you do if I brought Rosalita Gonzalez here to you?"

"Mr. Wells, go home to California. Make a report to the police in New Mexico, then go home to your daughter."

On the way back to headquarters, Deocampo took us on a detour, stopped the car downtown on Avenue 16 de Septiembre.

"Why are we stopped here?" I asked.

He pointed at a large three-story building. "See that?"

I looked at the building.

"The first two floors are a whorehouse."

"Thank you, but I'm good."

"On the third floor is the cartel, their offices."

"Like a drug cartel?"

"Exactly, a drug cartel." He put a cigarette in his mouth but did not light it. "That's what we deal with down here. The cartel has offices. You have a war on drugs, and we get shot. It is a mess. In Ciudad Juárez women are hunted. It didn't used to be like this. Maybe one day it will not be like this again."

"I'm sorry."

Deocampo shrugged. "Go home. You cannot save anybody. I cannot save anybody. Go home to your family."

a pocketknife, a tarp, a map, a compass, a shovel, a canteen, a poncho, a trail, a mission

Camaïeu

I drove home to my daughter.

I had been away from home for only weeks, but the strangeness of the house upon my return caused me to feel as if I had been gone for years. Like a coward sidling back onto a battlefield, I found all that I expected but cast in unfamiliar light, with unfamiliar and strange shadows. When I saw Meg's face, I wondered if she would ever again speak to me, but she did, her compassion, her love allowing her to understand that the grief I was experiencing was no less deep and intense than hers, that we each had to cope in our own way. My leaving, however, had cheated her out of an opportunity to run away as I had, to hide from the world that had been given to us.

She put to me a reasonable-enough question. "Where were you?"

"I told you, I was in New Mexico."

"What were you doing?"

I answered truthfully. "I don't know."

She nodded.

"Is Sarah asleep?"

"Yes. She went down easily."

"Has she asked for me?"

"No." That simple answer crushed me, but a yes would have been equally as devastating.

"Seizures?"

"A couple every day. There was a pretty severe one two days ago. Otherwise they've been mild. Spacing out." Meg began to cry.

I sat with her on the sofa, held her. We softened to each other in a way that we had not for some time.

Unusually progressive. That was how Dr. Gurewich characterized my daughter's condition. It sounded like a description of a private school. Unusually progressive. It was so much like falling. "Rapidly progressive dementia," Gurewich called it, sounding more distant and detached each time we consulted with her. Sarah hadn't known there was a ledge, and with just a few steps she was gone. But she was also there, present with me, in time and in space, in the same body, asleep at that moment while I sat in the chair beside her bed. Morning was just coming on, her shade up to allow the new light in. She was still beautiful, as she would forever be. She awoke and she recognized that it was morning, but there was nothing to indicate that she recognized me, yet she didn't recoil as if I were a stranger. She let me guide her to the bathroom. I stood with my back to her while she sat on the toilet and peed. The sound of her urine stopped, and I heard her frustration with the toilet paper. I turned to see her fumbling with the roll; she could not tear it off and hold it. I called out for Meg and then remembered she had gone out to yoga, finally some time for herself. The nurse had not yet arrived. Sarah looked at me, perhaps asking for help. I tore off some paper and wiped my daughter's vagina. When she was an infant, I changed her diaper so many times, being certain to dry inside her little creases. She didn't have a vagina then, not really, but now she was no infant. I had never felt so awkward, so scared, so inappropriate in my life, and yet I was performing this most intimate action for my dearest person. To feel so close to her while feeling so strange and weirdly guilty was confusing and disorienting. I happened to look at the tissue before tossing it into the bowl. The paper was tinged pink.

If my daughter had ever had a period, I didn't know about it. It was one of those things that as a father I was to know about and happily be unaware of. Here I was wiping my baby girl's vagina while wiping away evidence of her womanhood. I didn't know what to do. There were no pads within view in her bathroom, so I folded toilet paper until thick and pushed it against her and got some underwear on her. After I had pulled up her pajama bottoms and flushed the toilet, she looked at me and smiled.

"Are you all right?" she asked, sounding surprisingly collected.

"I'm fine," I said. "What about some breakfast?"

"That would be nice." Again, she sounded decidedly older, different from the little girl I remembered, and still there was no reason for me to assume she knew who I was.

"Do you know who I am?" I asked.

She ignored the question.

I got her into her robe and we moved to the kitchen, where I poured us bowls of cereal, Grape-Nuts. We sat beside each other at the table, facing the window and a view of the hills. Sarah managed to feed herself a couple of bites, and then she stopped eating, I thought, because of fear of attempting another. Her hands were failing her again.

Basil came over and pressed his head against Sarah's leg. She reached down and absently scratched him behind his ear. An automatic action that betrayed the person inside the shell. I was warmed by it, saddened by it.

"I know what," I said. "I'll be right back." I got up and went to the study, where I grabbed the board and chess pieces. At the table I was excited to see that Sarah recognized the board and the pieces. Though she fumbled with each one, she was able to place them correctly. She moved first. The game moved forward predictably, conservatively until she attempted to use a knight. She grabbed the horse and hovered it over the board, finally putting it down well away from any legal square.

I said nothing, didn't correct her, and went ahead and made my move.

She was somewhere else now. Whether it was a seizure, I didn't know. I sat with her, watching her, detecting a slight tremor in her right hand.

"Is it my move?" she asked.

"Yes."

"I'm tired. Daniel mopped the floor yesterday."

"He did?" I looked at the floor. I didn't know who Daniel was, but the floor was in need of mopping. "He did a good job," I lied.

"Daniel did it."

de dicto/de re

Of all possible worlds this was the one in which I had landed. I wondered how years passed for parents who lost children, how these parents navigated birthdays, Thanksgivings. Would my imaginary daughter grow older in my dreams? Would she graduate from high school and go to college? Have babies? Would my imagined child sit beside my deathbed and allow me to thank her for completing my world? However brief the time we shared. My daughter came to me in every nighttime dream, and I anticipated the self-loathing and guilt that would come years later when one night she would fail to appear, or rather, I would fail to conjure or summon her.

de se

Meg came into house through the kitchen door with a tray of two coffees and a paper sack of bagels. "Well, look who's up," she said.

Sarah got up and walked to Meg. "Thank you," she said, taking the bagels.

I glanced down at the chair beside me and noticed the blood-soaked cushion. "We have a small problem," I said.

At that moment Sarah turned away from Meg to move to the counter. Meg saw the child's blood-stained pants.

"I didn't know quite how to handle it," I said.

Meg put her hands on Sarah's shoulders and tried to gently guide her out of the room. Sarah resisted, twisting away, shaking her head. Meg tried again.

"No," Sarah said. She bent slightly at the waist, perhaps cramping. I didn't know.

Meg's eyes welled up. She tried again.

I stood but didn't move forward.

Sarah looked at me. She was shaking. "What are you going to do?" she asked. She looked so frightened to me that I was near crying as well.

Meg made soothing sounds. "It's okay, baby. We just need to go back to the bathroom and get more comfortable. That's a good idea, isn't it?" She did not push or pull but touched Sarah's face. "Is that a good idea?"

Sarah nodded.

I sat like a dumb bird at the table. A pigeon, perhaps, or a chicken. I considered my beautiful daughter marking this change in her physical development while being completely unaware of her body or herself, with no attendant fears that she might have had in a more normal world, while the fabric of her understanding of the most basic, ever-taken-for-granted truths about daily life frayed not only at the edges but from the middle, spiderwebbing out, growing and connecting one destruction to the next. My daughter, a little life in the scheme of the world, of time, the star, however, around which my planet orbited. My source of gravity and warmth and light was eroding and so was I, and I could not help her, couldn't even contact her to offer an apology or say good-bye or express my love. There might not have been the heaven that so many fools advertised, but there certainly was a hell, and it smelled like blood and cold cereal and the family dog.

I called Basil to me and let him comfort me. The way he settled his chin on my thigh let me know that I was also comforting him. I moved the stained chair cushion into the laundry room.

Meg came back into the kitchen with Sarah in fresh clothes, sweatpants and a yellow T-shirt. The child returned to her previous seat, minus cushion, and fiddled with the pieces on the board with no seeming notion of a game or a promise of one.

I pulled a chair out for Meg and sat where I had been.

"That was her first," she said. She did not cry now, but the look on her face could easily have been wailing.

"Who is Daniel?" I asked.

"Daniel?"

"Sarah said Daniel mopped the floor."

Meg shrugged. What else could she do. These behaviors were in line with what the doctor had told us. She had even said there might be fits of paranoia or rage. The mere thought sent me into panic.

"What time does the nurse get here?" I asked.

"She's not coming. She called to say she had an emergency."

"I like that better," I said. "I'm here all day today. You can go out and do what you need to."

"There are pads in our bathroom," she said.

"What?"

"Pads. For Sarah."

"Right."

Meg nodded. She turned to look out the window. A Steller's jay was on a branch of the jacaranda. It was unusual for one to come so far down.

There were times in life that things felt easy and slow, or easy and fast, somehow not the world of grown-ups, but everything now felt so hard, so real, every move an effort and a mystery, yet strangely, no move seemed as if it could be wrong. How could things be worse? I watched like a big cat for any flicker of joy or mere recognition on my child's face, ready to pounce on it and stretch it out in front of me.

fac et spera

I spent the day trying to keep my daughter alive. It was just like when she was the infant we brought home. I couldn't believe the people at the hospital were just letting us leave with that little animal. They made sure we had a car seat, presented us with a cheap stroller, and sent us on our way. I also could not believe that Meg was walking, now sitting in the backseat with the strapped-in infant, after having just pushed a person out of her body. It was all so surreal. It remained surreal when we arrived home. The surreality either faded or became the norm as the days passed and we became used to it all, but now all was as surreal as it ever was.

We sat around the house. I read to her. We watched cartoons that Sarah had long outgrown, it being unclear whether she was watching or seizing. I even managed to steer her through a short walk along a short and easy trail along the bottom of the mountain. When we returned, a bit hot and sweaty from the early summer heat, I left her in the kitchen while I went to pee. I was gone for only a minute. I returned to find Sarah sitting on the floor, loving up on Basil. The sight made me feel an inkling of happiness. Then I heard a humming. It was coming from the microwave. The light was on, and through the glass I could see a mug full of forks spinning clockwise on the table. I don't know if I saw a spark or not, but I certainly imagined one, if not many, as I leaped to open the door. My heart was racing.

I thought I heard Sarah say, "Daddy." When I turned, however, she was still focused on the dog and didn't show any sign of having even noticed me. That word from her lips had been the most beautiful music of my life, and now I knew that I would probably never hear it again.

Meg returned. We spent a quiet day with our daughter. I told her about the microwave, and we now knew we could not leave Sarah alone even for a minute. We ate. We went to bed. We, Meg and I, lay side by side, with nothing to say. There was nothing to say. Until Meg said the right thing.

"I love you," she said.

"Thank you," I said. "I love you too."

In my dream, Hilary Gill was smoking a cigarette and clearly not enjoying it. She grimaced with every drag and coughed when she exhaled blue clouds that sank to her skirted knees. Perhaps the most significant thing was that she was alive, a fact that was not lost on dream Hilary Gill.

"Why a doornail?" she asked. She was fiddling with a laptop computer on her lap, trying to adjust the screen so that she could see.

"What?" I asked.

"A doornail? What's a nail have to do with death? 'Dead as a doornail,' they say. What is a doornail, anyway?"

"It's a long nail that was once used to fasten the parts of a door together," I said. I was seated at a table not far from her. I was surprised to find myself talking.

"What's it got to do with dead?" she asked. "Or death?"

"It was driven all the way through, and the point was pounded over and back into the wood so that it could not be pulled out, and so it was called 'dead.'"

"That's stupid," she said.

"Well, there you have it."

"Fieldwork is the best part, don't you think?" Hilary Gill asked.

"The best part of what?" I asked.

"Of what we do. Oh, the teaching is okay, a little tiring, boring.

The administrative shit is easy enough but mind-numbing. The committee work is something Stalin dreamed up, I'm sure. And the publishing just to publish, that's sick. Who the fuck cares about any of this shit? Who does it make a difference to?"

"I suppose. It's all part of a conversation, isn't it?" I asked. I felt like a wide-eyed kid, and perhaps I was.

Hilary Gill laughed. "I never pegged you for being so naive." She pulled long and hard on the cigarette and made that face. "Sorry about your daughter."

I shrugged.

"You should have fucked me while you had the chance."

"What?"

"You should have fucked me. Then right now you could really feel like shit, even more than you do. You'd be losing your child and you'd feel guilty for driving me to suicide by fucking me and then by not fucking me again. A perfect guilt storm."

"I never wanted to fuck you," I said.

"It's okay to admit it."

"I never wanted to fuck you," I repeated.

"That hurts," she said, a blue cloud falling from her lips. "No wonder I killed myself. Do you know what I mean?"

"I suppose."

She pushed her cigarette out on her palm and did not grimace. "And why was Lisbon worthy of such treatment and misery?" she said. "Like Voltaire, I hold contempt for such a god. To hell with Leibniz, that suck-up. And can you then impute a sinful deed? This, the best of all possible worlds. All for the best. God knows. It's a mystery. His will. Ha! An absentee landlord at best. To babes who on their mothers' bosoms bleed?"

I listened to dream-dead Hilary Gill and was willing to accept her as a ghost in my world, even if I didn't know what she was talking about. However, it being my dream, my construction, I, logically, necessarily, must have understood her message.

"Was there more vice in fallen Lisbon found?" she asked.

The nurse's name was Kendall. I cannot say that I liked her very much upon meeting her. She was a young white woman with a sleeve of tattoos that interested me little beyond their mere color. There might have been a panda bear. She seemed competent enough. After all, she wasn't there to stimulate my daughter, to teach her anything, to enrich her experience of the world. She was there to wipe her ass, feed her, and now, apparently, to keep her from burning down the house. I was disappointed in myself that her lack of education caused me to dismiss her. Perhaps it was that I could too easily imagine her as a girlfriend to one of the white militia members from the compound in New Mexico.

Had Sarah responded to her in any way, I might have felt differently. I looked to see any kind of variation in my child's expression. Sadly, Kendall's face was as blank as Sarah's without the excuse of dementia. Then it occurred to me that I was looking to simply blame some body for some thing, which was slightly different from blaming somebody for something. Kendall followed Sarah around while I sat in various rooms of the house pretending to read or make notes, pretending as much for myself as anyone else. I was free to leave the house but found I could not.

On the desk in my study I had laid out the notes from New Mexico, and on a sheet of white paper I had mindlessly written again and again "Rosalita Gonzalez." I could see the woman's face as clearly as her name written in front of me. She had dark, defined eyebrows set above narrow, light brown eyes. Her face was round, like the faces of many pictures of Inuit women I had seen in books. Her skin was the light brown of my daughter's skin. She had a scar on her forehead, left middle. Her teeth were straight, I knew, though I had not seen her smile.

I heard raised voices from the kitchen and stood, as if that made my hearing more acute. It was Sarah. "Keep her away from me!" she shouted. I walked to the kitchen.

"It's okay, sweetie," Meg said. She was standing by the open back door.

Kendall was standing near the counter between Meg and Sarah, who was at the table, supporting herself with her hand on the edge of it. I was surprised to discover that she was screaming at her mother.

"Who is she? What do you want?" Sarah said.

"That's your mother," Kendall said. Her voice was such a strange monotone that even I wouldn't have believed her.

Sarah looked at me. "Help me, Daniel!"

I looked at Meg's terrified face.

Sarah ran to me, hugged me around my waist. As she did, I realized who Daniel was. When she was a child, I had made up a string of stories that included my made-up friend Daniel. Daniel was constantly saving me from peril.

Meg was crying now. She turned and walked out of the house, leaving the back door open.

That night I sat alone with Sarah at the kitchen window. Even now that construction haunts me, that I sat alone while being with my daughter. The moon was full and bright and within easy view. I at least imagined a fleeting flash of joy on her face as she stared at it. I attended to my own breathing, trying to calm myself. The thought that my daughter was so very far away from herself rattled me profoundly. If I hadn't focused on breathing, I might simply have stopped.

simula me cognoscere

The campus had that quiet summer personality that faculty seemed to love. Perhaps it was time to focus on research, starting or completing. More likely it was mere reprieve, the welcome lull following exhaustion and preceding exertion. Regardless, whether it made sense or not, the campus minus the students offered a certain kind of peace. I went there, ostensibly to work on a couple of articles that had hopelessly stalled. I managed somehow to convince myself that I was actually interested in my own research, but I was in no way oblivious to the fact that work was just another escape from my woes at home.

I wandered across campus to my favorite coffee shop for a blueberry muffin at lunchtime. On my way back, I walked past Hilary Gill's office. The door was open. The room had been cleared of all of her belongings, her books, her tchotchkes, and had been expertly cleaned. The surfaces were spotless and wet looking under the lights that had been left on. It looked as if the place had been cleansed of her blood and breath. I supposed that it had been just that. It occurred to me that I didn't know how young Gill had killed herself. I never asked anyone, never read about it, and, frankly, didn't care to know. It was tragic that her life had become so difficult, but no life is required to continue; no life will continue forever. I hoped that she had found what she wanted, what she needed. I lost my desire to work and packed up my notes.

I ran into Finley Huckster as I exited the building.

"Hot enough for you?" he asked. "Don't you hate it when people say that?"

"Yeah, it's hot enough."

"How is the summer treating you? How's your daughter?"

"She's having a rough time." I was very close to telling him that she had died, but somehow, true as it may have seemed, it felt like a betrayal. "We're dealing with it."

"I'm sorry."

"Thanks, Huck."

"What are you up to? Feel like a game of squash?"

"Not today." I looked past him across the sparely populated campus. "I have an appointment downtown."

"Some other time."

"You bet."

"You know, anytime you want to talk."

"Thanks, Huck. How's your family?"

"All fine."

"Well, squash next week," I said.

"Definitely."

Little was as depressing as a downtown bar at three in the afternoon. One couldn't have the excuse of seeking out mixed nuts and popcorn as a lunchtime snack. One was too early for so-called happy hour. So, the visit was either the product of depression or of a planned meeting that needn't be talked about. My tavern of choice, a loose term—choice, not tavern—was on Fourth Street just east of Spring, just a couple of blocks from skid row. I had always admired the keyhole-shaped entry and the door that didn't quite close tightly. The last time I was there, I ended up in a fight. That was perhaps my ambition that afternoon. The bartender gave me a long look like he might have remembered me. If he did, he didn't say anything and apparently gave me no further thought. I was the only pathetic patron in the pathetic place, but still he gave me my space, either fixing or pretending to fix the soda machine.

I nursed the same cheap scotch and ice for twenty minutes. Finally, the bartender came back to me. "Are you waiting for somebody?"

"That's actually none of your business," I said. I was an asshole. I wanted to get my ass kicked, wanted the same guys from that evening months earlier to come in and beat me up.

Another twenty minutes passed. A woman came in. I was fairly certain she was a prostitute, but I really didn't know. I had no street smarts to speak of. Whatever she was, she showed absolutely no interest in me. Perhaps I looked like a cop. Not likely. It was more likely that I appeared to her as a khaki-and-Oxford-shirt-wearing serial killer. She parked herself in a corner booth without ordering anything.

I slapped a sizable tip on the bar and waved to the bartender. "I'm sorry I was such an asshole."

"It's okay, buddy. That's why we're open." He was smarter than I had given him credit for.

Walking the hot and dirty three blocks back to the outdoor lot where I had parked my car, I felt a sense of dread about going home, a dread different from the standard, run-of-the-mill dread. I found I was fidgeting. I seldom if ever fidgeted. I tapped my car keys inside my pants pocket, played with my watchband, pulled the flesh of my thumbs away from my nails with the sides of my index fingers. I sat behind the wheel in the sauna that was my Jeep until the elderly attendant apparently took note and, afraid that I would die and stink up the place, called the police.

scio nomen meum

Basil was barking. Basil never barked. I hurried across the drive to the back door. There was no sound but Basil's barking, a high-pitched complaint that made him sound younger. Inside, I very nearly collided with Meg's back. Beyond her, facing her, was Sarah, wild eyed and shaking, holding a carving knife by the blade. Blood was pouring from her palm.

"Daniel," she said to me, "who is she?!"

"It's your mother, baby," I said.

"Daniel?"

I walked toward her. I could feel Meg trembling as I brushed past her. "Yes, Sarah. It's me, Daniel."

"Why?" she asked. There were so many levels to her question. I was asking why as well. Was she asking why she was fading? Why she was dying? Why her parents were strange to her and so afraid?

"I don't know why, baby." I stepped closer. I needed to get the knife out of her hand.

Meg was audibly crying now.

"Let me have the knife, Sarah. That belongs to me."

She spaced out. She was having a seizure. I moved quickly to her, pried open her fingers, and removed the blade. "Get a towel," I said to Meg.

Meg moved quickly.

The blade had gone nearly halfway through her index, middle, and ring fingers. The blood was flowing freely. Meg handed me a towel and wrapped the hand up. "I'll hold her hand. You drive."

Meg was in her robe, but she ran in front of me while I carried Sarah. I sat in the backseat of Meg's car, holding our daughter firmly, fearing her coming to from the seizure. That return started with a small start, a kick of her leg. She closed then opened her eyes, tried to figure out where she was. She looked at my face, and I thought I detected a flash of recognition, but then she caught sight of the blood-soaked towel wrapped around her hand. Whether it was the sight or the sensation of pain that found its way to her I didn't know, but she issued the first breath of a scream before passing out. Perhaps she passed out because of a loss of blood. I didn't know, and it was all so terrifying. Meg ran red lights, leaned forward toward the steering wheel, but said nothing. We arrived at the Huntington Hospital emergency room and I carried Sarah in. The sight of the unconscious child and the copious amount of blood prompted swift attention. If we attracted reproving glances, I was unaware of them. The doctors set to work on Sarah's hand. We answered all health questions and described the incident. Only then did a nurse raise an eyebrow, but another nurse heard the word *Batten* and erased the concern of child abuse from the room.

While we waited, Meg in her robe, I in blood, we somehow managed a call to Gurewich, and, to our surprise, she was there in short order. She made clear that there was nothing she could do, but she wanted to be there for us. I amused myself with the thought that people often make a point of declaring their uselessness in order to be helpful. *I can't change anything, but I'm here for you.* Still, her presence provided some kind of comfort.

Meg described everything to Gurewich.

"It will not get better," the doctor said. "It is possible that there will be moments of lucidity. Dementia is a mystery, and it manifests very differently in people, especially in children. I know that this was terrifying for you."

"That's an understatement," I said. I reached over and put my hand on Meg's. "What do we do? The paranoia is too much."

It was clear that what Gurewich was going to say next was difficult for her. "You need to consider placing Sarah in a care facility."

That had of course crossed my mind, but I couldn't maintain the thought, and I certainly hadn't shared it with Meg. I appreciated that Gurewich had used my daughter's name, that she had not reduced Sarah to a mere pronoun.

transit lux, umbra permanet

Sarah had suffered severe nerve and tendon damage, and even after surgery it was unclear how much of the impairment would be permanent, but all of that was so tragically moot. Sarah herself would never be *permanent*. That was the real sadness of seeing her hand so encased and held in that restraint against her flat little chest, that any incapacitation was really meaningless, hardly an inconvenience. She had said nothing, made no sound, lucid or otherwise, since the frantic drive to the emergency room. In fact, there was no evidence that she was even aware of any difference in her being, except that she was clearly confused by being constrained from free movement.

The idea of making arrangements for care, the task of locating and contacting a facility that was acceptable, seemed, in the abstract, nearly impossible, but when confronted with stark truth, real life, it had to happen, and so it did. We found a place that was not so far from us near the town of Sierra Madre, set up against the foothills just as we were. I imagined that the similar and familiar setting might provide some level of comfort for my daughter.

The staff was kind enough, if understandably numb to our situation, or any, for that matter. Sarah's room looked like any boarding school dorm room, except that it was conspicuously missing any hard edges. The head- and footboards of the bed were curved and upholstered. The one small table was, of course, round, made of wood with a vinyl bumper along its circumference. The name of the place was at once innocuous and portentous, perhaps even ill omened.

A middle-aged Korean woman named May managed the place. She was perhaps the most positive human being I had ever met. If she had possessed a tail, it would have wagged nonstop. Instead she possessed a wide smile that was so bright it seemed creepy. For a moment I wondered if her electricity might even cure my daughter, but only for a moment. She did lean close and talk to Sarah like she was the person she was. She did that every time.

"Are we not hungry today?" May asked when the food would fall from her slack lips. "That's okay, dear. Sometimes I'm not hungry too."

I came to sit with Sarah and found May in the room, holding her good hand, smiling. She remained for a while after my arrival, her little belly pushing into her lap.

"She had a good night," May said.

I wondered what that meant. It was clear that May was moved by the fact that Sarah was a child. There were no other children in the facility as far as I could see.

"My daughter died when she was seven," May said.

"I'm sorry," I said.

"That was thirty-one years ago. Cancer."

"Does it get easier?"

She looked down at her knees for a second, then at my eyes. "No."

I nodded.

"She's in there," May said.

I could see the Jesus on her sleeve. It didn't offend me or even put me off. It was, in its way, sweet. "Thank you, May. I'm sure your daughter is still with you."

"No, she's not," she said, flatly. With that she got up, smiled, and walked out.

When May was gone from the room, I looked at my daughter and realized that she had disappeared during my brief conversation, that, in fact, she, Sarah, was not in the room and not in that small body, had not been there, would not be there. While I watched her, she experienced a seizure; it hardly mattered. I wiped her lips and chin clean with a white cotton towel.

Meg blamed herself for Sarah's wound and, I believe, somehow worked that into blame for her condition. It was irrational, fairly obvious to anyone outside her head, but real and effective enough. We might have survived our daughter's death, but the process of her dying was killing us, certainly driving us apart. We took turns sitting with Sarah and were almost never there together. Weeks passed.

Months passed. Sarah faded more. Even May's smile faded. The sun remained bright every day. The moon moved around the sky. And I continued to sit in that room, now in a recliner beside my daughter's bed or wheelchair.

One Wednesday I glanced out the window and saw a shadow. It was high noon and sunny. A young bear had come down from the mountain. He had found the red sugar water of a hummingbird feeder and was sitting on his fat ass, lapping it up. The sight was a joyous one for me; it was the bear that Sarah had been looking for her entire life. I pushed her chair to the window. I looked at my daughter's empty eyes. I looked at the bear. It was so big, so real, so alive. I put my arms around my child and cried. "Please, see the bear, baby. Please."

I weighed close to two hundred pounds. I had large hands. The thread count of the bedding in Sarah's room could not have been better than 180. It felt a little scratchy against my palms. The fabric of the pillow slip was not slippery at all. Sarah didn't move much. She never moved much. She would never again move much, move at all. I told my daughter I loved her. She knew that I loved her.

As I left the building, May gave me a long look, offered a gentle smile.

"There was a bear outside," I said.

"I saw him," she said. "Is she sleeping?"

"She is."

"I'll just let her rest then."

"Thank you, May."

ursa

the bird flies out;
the bird flies back again

It was hotter in New Mexico.

The names Jeff and Roger somehow didn't fit them. Conway and Chet seemed too over the top. Braden and Don sounded about right. But, alas, they were Jeff and Roger, an understated Mutt and Jeff. Jeff brightened on finding me in the diner. A worried DeLois gave us space.

"I thought you went and ran out on us," he said as they both sat across from me in the booth. I replayed his utterance in my head. Conway was not over the top.

"No, I just had to run some numbers, check in at the office, visit my girlfriend." DeLois delivered my coffee.

"Bring me a coffee," Jeff said without looking at her.

"Dr. Pepper for me, please," Roger said. The *please* sounded like a foreign language in his mouth. He might as well have said *bitte*.

"So, what's the word?" Jeff asked.

"Don't know yet," I said.

"Yes, you do."

"No, I don't." I paused for dramatic effect. "It's looking good."

Jeff slapped Mutt with the back of his hand. "So, you need to come back out for more tests?"

"Maybe. I'm still waiting for some test results. Other people need to interpret the readings I've already taken." I hoped he wouldn't ask for details.

"And we're getting the news first, right?"

"As first as I can manage."

"So, what do I do?"

I shrugged.

They stood. "We're good, right?" Jeff said.

"We're good," I said.

When they were gone, DeLois came to my table with a free piece of pie, slid it in front of me.

"What's this?"

"What are you doing?" she asked.

I stared at her.

"Are you a cop or something?"

"No, DeLois, I'm no cop. I'm just a geologist."

"Yeah, right," she said. "I don't know what you're up to, but you'd better be careful. Those good old boys will kill you in a second."

I nodded. "Thanks for the concern." I looked across at the post office. "Have you ever seen the school bus they drive?"

"Yes." Her tone changed, became quieter.

"You've seen the women?"

"Yes."

"Let me ask you this: How often do the cops drive by here?" I asked.

"Every now and again. Just one comes around. He likes to talk to Jeff and the stupid one when he's here."

"Is that right?"

"That's right."

"Thanks for the pie," I said.

"I hope you know what you're doing."

"So do I."

I ate my pie and got up to leave.

"Thursdays," DeLois said.

"Excuse me?"

"That's when the bus comes by. I don't know where they're going."

"Thank you, DeLois."

As I was getting into my Jeep, DeLois came trotting after me.

"Did I forget something?" I asked.

"I get off at six," she said.

"What?"

"I get off at six. I'll make you dinner."

"I don't know," I said. I looked at her face. She had a kind face. "Okay. I'll be back here at six."

It was hotter in New Mexico.

DeLois's last name was McIntosh. I learned this because it was written on a notebook on the floor of her older, nondescript Japanese sedan. Below her name, in the same loopy cursive, was the word *poetry*. She caught me looking down at it.

"I take a class once a week up in Albuquerque."

"That's good."

She insisted on driving instead of having me follow. Because of the many turns to her place, she claimed I'd never find my way back. She would bring me back to my car.

"Taking classes is a good thing," I said.

"You haven't read my poetry," she said. "And you're not going to. It ain't fit for human consumption."

"I'm sure that's not true."

"Anyway, I like the class. Do you teach at a college? You just seem like a teacher at a college."

"I do."

"What?"

"Geology."

"Professor," she said. "So, where did you disappear to? I didn't think you were coming back. And you didn't say good-bye."

"I had to go to a funeral."

"I'm sorry."

I looked out the window. The landscape was still fully lit. "This is actually a pretty place," I said.

She laughed. "You're either taking too many of those pills or not enough." She turned off the highway onto a gravel road. "Are you married?"

"Yes."

"What does your wife do?"

"She's a college teacher too. She's a poet."

"No shit. Do you like her poetry?"

No one had ever asked me that before, and I was caught a little off guard. "I can't honestly say I understand it."

"So no."

"I don't understand it, anyway. I'll leave it at that. I'm just a scientist."

What seemed like a half dozen more turns convinced me that she had been right about driving. We ended up in a high-walled canyon on a dirt road that looked like it had been made for flooding. I recalled DeLois telling me that her husband or boyfriend had left on a run to the store and had never come back. I considered that maybe he was just lost.

The cabin was nestled against an outcropping of rocks that seemed geologically out of place. There was a wraparound porch and a garden and the only tree for miles, a small desert willow that she had obviously planted.

"Nice tree," I said.

"It struggles," she said.

"You have power out here?"

"Generator."

I had always envied people who lived off the grid. I was impressed by DeLois.

"I inherited this little getaway from my father. He was a rough old son of a bitch. The real deal."

"I guess so."

"There is a well," she said. "So I don't have to go traipsing out in my altogether to do my whatever."

"You're a natural poet," I said.

The interior of the house was clean and modest, colorful. She asked that I remove my shoes at the door.

"I really like your house," I told her. "It reminds me of you."

"You don't even know me."

"I know a little," I said.

"We're having salad," she said. "And corn."

"Sounds good."

"You can look at the house while I chop. That will take you all of thirty seconds."

To be polite I made a sweep through the house. It was a home. A neat, clean home. I returned to the kitchen and was put to work chopping carrots and fennel.

"So, who died?" DeLois asked.

"A family member."

DeLois dropped the corn into the boiling water and looked at me for a second. "Why are you here?"

"You invited me."

"In New Mexico?"

"Looking for oil."

She leaned back against the sink and stared at me.

"What do you want me to say?"

She continued to stare.

"I'm here because of the women on the bus."

She was listening.

I knew that my retelling would be nothing but confusing, so I went for concision. "Those poor women are being held as slaves."

"How do you know that?"

"I know it. They told me. How I know is complicated. I have to do something, but I don't know what."

"I told you not to fuck with those guys. They scare the shit out of me."

"Me too."

"Call the cops."

"The story of how I know about the women is complicated and sounds crazy. And I'm not sure I can trust the police. I actually went to Ciudad Juárez and talked to the police. One of the women is from there. Her name is Rosalita Gonzalez."

"You're certain about all of this?" she said.

"I am."

"So, what are you going to do?" I could hear the fear in her voice.

"I don't know. Maybe nothing," I said.

We ate our meal sitting on her maroon velour sofa. There was little relief from the heat until the sun was gone. The windows were all open. I was surprised to see bats in the darkening sky. I said as much.

"They get in here sometimes," she said. "I just shoo them out. What's a little rabies between friends?"

If I hadn't liked DeLois before, I liked her now. Truth was, I had liked her from the beginning. At that moment, her smile reminded me of May's smile. I recalled the slight nod and acknowledgment or approval or understanding that she had given me as I left the facility that night. DeLois's smile, like May's, didn't so much offer optimism as it simply, merely offered. So we ate, the bats outside with the calls of chat-littles.

I heard stories about DeLois's parents, especially her father. About her job, a necessity. About her classes. Ceramics, the evidence of which surrounded us. Macramé. Refrigerator repair.

"Really?"

"Yes. I've fixed the unit in the diner twice already. I can work on my car too. You have to be self-sufficient out here."

"I'm impressed."

"I want to help," she said.

"Excuse me?"

"With the women. Let me help."

"Help me with what? Why?"

"It's easy enough to become alone in the world. Even without living way out here like I do." She touched my hand.

"You should drive me back," I said.

"You don't have to leave."

"You should drive me back."

And so she did.

I called Meg and we struggled through a tense silence.

"What are you doing?" she asked.

"I don't know," I said. "I'm sorry. I just have to be alone. Are you all right?" It was a stupid question.

"Are you coming home?"

"Yes. I love you, Meg."

She said nothing.

"I'll be home soon."

She hung up.

To say that I felt bad was an understatement. I rationalized my indulgence by thinking that everyone has to process grief in her or his own way. The rationalization was yet another indulgence. I tried to sleep. I'm quite certain I did. And I probably dreamed. And I was probably disturbed by those dreams. Probably.

Once again in my dingy little Motel 6 room, I stared at the ceiling while listening to the loop of CNN, hearing but not acknowledging that the world was happening someplace else. I consumed a lot of the foods I would never let my daughter eat. Stress eating, boredom eating, whatever, it was the kind of mindless eating that would make me fat and eventually dead. *Tell everybody I'm drinking again / Doctor said it'd kill me, but he didn't say when.*

I set the thermostat on the noisy unit below the window cold enough that I could pull the blanket and sheet over me, as if I needed some kind of layer between me and whatever else there was. It was Monday night. In three days it would be Thursday.

It was hotter in New Mexico.

I found the Quebradas backcountry road just north of Socorro off the interstate. It was early morning. I crossed the Rio Grande and imagined crossing it at another point south soon enough. I passed through the collection of modest buildings that was the still-sleeping village of Pueblito. It felt good to have the Jeep off the highway and on a trail. It gave me a sense of solitude, though I was anything but alone. I drove slowly, wondering just what I was going to do. It would have been easy enough to pack up and drive home to Los Angeles, but I knew I wouldn't do that, couldn't do that. As I drove deeper into a temporary nowhere, I was more relaxed, my breathing found a familiar rhythm, and I saw the landscape more clearly. The colors out there were deep browns, reds, ochre; "a desert rainbow," I had once heard it called. The cactuses were past blooming but beautiful nonetheless. I imagined seeing it all with Sarah. And then with Meg. I realized that I still loved my wife, and yet here I was, having left her all alone. All alone. So that I might do something good? So that I might in some way redeem myself? I hated the notion of redemption. But here I was in the world, in this world. I would do something.

I stopped and walked out through the cholla and ocotillos. It was already extremely hot. I was certain that to someone flying overhead or driving by I looked like the ridiculous cliché of a scientist or ranger, clad all in khaki, long pants and sleeves to protect me from the harsh sun. Perhaps to protect me from the bright light of God. If there was a God, he or she was no good at its job. Apparently there was just too much to do, listening to the prayers of all those who actually mattered, the faithful, the pious, the deluded, the stupid. My clumsy, unmeasured strides brought me too close to a rattlesnake. I saw him before he needed to warn me, but still we eyed each other warily as I steered wide of him. I wondered if maybe he was God, out for a walk (or a slither) just like me, through the peace and solitude of the desert. I took a knee and examined the tracks of what I thought was a kit fox. Maybe she was God. God had to be somewhere, why not lost in that desert? That would explain a lot.

I returned to my Jeep and drove to the end of the trail. It was only midday. I drove north on what I believed was an old dirt mining road. It was arrow straight for five miles, then turned east for a mile, where the road hit a primitive trail that looked more like a rocky wash than anything. I was reminded of a time when I followed directions to a high mountain lake farther north in New Mexico. I was told it was good I had four-wheel drive and that turned out to be true, as I climbed over boulders and straddled deep ruts. I didn't see another car during the thirty minutes it took me to drive five miles. When I arrived, however, I found the lakeshore peppered with cars, regular cars, Pintos and Datsuns and Chevy Vegas. The sight was so astonishing that I asked a woman who sat fishing if there was another road up to the place. She gave me a look, a mildly interested look, and said, "No, only the one."

I followed the primitive trail south and hoped that it would not rain. Rain would have been a disaster. The road never got better and actually petered out completely as the hillside flattened, just when a highway came into sight. When I got to the road, I realized it was, in fact, 380, the road that had taken me so many times now from San Antonio to Bingham and on to the Nazis' compound. I had come full circle; it seemed I could not escape.

I drove past the diner, hoping that DeLois would not see me pass, on to the turn left to the compound. I drove past it up the hill far enough that I could park behind a bluff and remain unnoticed. I watched the Nazis through my field glasses. I thought of my friend who had died in that helicopter crash in the Canyon.

I watched for a long hour under that sun, consumed the last of my water, and finally gave up. Nothing happened down there. I at least could have found some interesting Nazis, some industrious ones, but aside from the keeping of slaves, they bored me to death. Why weren't they building an armored personnel vehicle or a ballistic missile? Instead they were inside their little house eating bologna sandwiches or having a circle jerk. Still, my Nazis scared me.

It was hotter in New Mexico.

The knock at the door came as I was drifting off to sleep and scared me near to death. I considered not opening the door. If I had had a usable window in the washroom, I would have climbed through it. DeLois's voice poked through my haze of fear and I came around. I still held grave reservations about opening the door, but I did. I did and I found DeLois and five other people, three women and two men, all looking rather serious.

"DeLois, what are you doing here?" I asked.

"We're here to help."

I gave the parking lot a quick survey. "Come in."

They walked in and stood by the round table by the window.

"How did you find me?"

"Your Jeep. There are only two motels in town," DeLois said.

"And I know the manager," a short, round white woman said. Her hair was done up in a tight gray bun.

"Who are you people?" I asked. I might have sounded irritated, but I was more confused than anything else.

"They're from my poetry workshop," DeLois said.

"Poets?" I stepped back and sat on the nearer of two beds. "Could you all just go home?"

"We want to help." This from a tall, lean young man I thought might be Hispanic or maybe Native.

"What's your name?" I asked.

They took this as an invitation to introduce themselves.

"I'm Jaime," the young man said.

"Grace," from a tall black woman with braids.

"Rosalva." She was extremely short, the youngest looking. She wore platform boots that were at least four inches high.

"Ernesto." A Hispanic man about my age with an impressive salt-and-pepper mustache. He wore a Desert Storm jacket.

"Georgia," from the old woman with the gray bun. I looked at her concho belt and wide skirt and thought, Of course.

"You don't understand," I said. "I don't want to know you people. I need for you to go away."

"This Thursday?" DeLois asked.

"What?" I shook my head.

"Are we doing this or not?" from Ernesto.

"Where are we taking them?" Georgia asked.

"The police," Rosalva said.

Jaime laughed. "We can't trust the police."

"The police in Albuquerque," Rosalva said.

"Can't trust any police," the young man said. "That one, Jeff, he used to be a cop over in Belen."

Everyone was silent for a few seconds.

"So, no cops," Jaime said.

"He's right," DeLois said. "No cops of any kind."

"What about the tribal police?" Georgia asked.

"He goes fishing on Thursday," Ernesto said.

They all laughed.

"We really can help," DeLois said. She walked over to the coffee maker and grabbed the pot, stepped into the washroom, and filled it at the sink.

"Help with what?"

"I know what you're up to," she said. "Why else would you be here? You left and then you came back. I don't know what your story is, but you're doing the right thing. We all think you're doing the right thing."

"And what is that?"

"You know."

"Maybe we can hide them in our homes," Grace said.

"Fifteen of them?" Ernesto said.

"Not a good idea," Rosalva said.

Jaime turned, pulled back the curtain, and looked out at the parking lot. "Those are some nasty dudes. Bad motherfuckers."

"Jaime," Georgia said, objecting to his language.

"Well, they are," Jaime said. "They scare the shit out of me. They're KKK or something. Nazis. They wouldn't think twice about killing any one of us."

"That's true," Georgia said.

"Mexico," I said. I couldn't believe I was hearing my own voice. I felt I had either surprised myself or betrayed myself.

They looked at me, confused by my having spoken.

"What?" from Ernesto.

"Mexico," I repeated.

"That's brilliant," Georgia said.

"How many are there?" DeLois asked.

"I don't know. Twelve, fifteen." I couldn't believe I was talking to them. "It doesn't matter. We're not doing anything."

We sat for what seemed like a long time without speaking. Finally, DeLois asked, "How many men were with them last time?"

"Two," I said. "I saw two."

Another silence.

"I'll need to take their bus," I said.

It was hotter in New Mexico.

The next day I found Lieutenant Deocampo's telephone number and called him. He answered and was clearly surprised to hear from me.

"Señor Wells, how are you?"

"I've been better. If I come to the border with some refugees, will you take them?"

"Refugees?"

"Rosalita Gonzalez and some others."

"What exactly are you saying, señor Wells?"

"I am bringing Mexican citizens across the border. They have been held captive here, and I am bringing them to Ciudad Juárez. Will you meet me there?"

There was a long pause on the other end.

"Lieutenant Deocampo?"

"Sí?"

"I'm not crazy," I said.

"I know that."

"Okay. So, will you be there?"

"When?"

"Tomorrow. I don't know what time."

"How many?"

"I'm not sure. Maybe thirteen, fourteen. Does that matter?"

"How are you moving that many people?" he asked.

"Will you meet us?"

"Are you in danger?" he asked. "You should call the police." He listened to my silence. "Señor Wells?"

"I'll call you with a time."

"Señor Wells?"

"Lieutenant?"

"Ten ciudado, mi amigo."

"Thank you."

In my dream I was climbing a steep mountain face, rocky with patches of ice here and there. I was driving pitons, tying knots, snapping in carabiners, the whole deal, but I had never climbed in my life. So, even as I went about my business as if I knew what I was doing, what I was doing was absolute nonsense. It soon became clear to me that I didn't even know whether I was going up or down the mountain. I was climbing with a man who looked very familiar, but I did not know him. I wondered, there in my dream, if it was possible to know someone in a dream whom I did not know in my waking life. What would it have meant to recognize my companion? While I was thinking about that, all of the pitons popped out of the face, all of the knots untied, all of the carabiners snapped open, and suddenly we were falling, side by side, into the abyss. My unknown friend looked at me, smiled, and said, "All I can tell is that gravity is a motherfucker."

"True enough," I said.

"That and God hates me," he said.

"Hate him back," I said.

The rain fell nearly every afternoon. Thunderheads would form over the mountains and collect through the day. The lightning was in the air, to be felt even when you couldn't see it flashing. But it also flashed, sometimes as great, wide sheets of white and at others like the cliché bolts of Tesla's coil. It would have been comforting to connect the power to some, well, power, but it was merely electricity. As beautiful and as dangerous as it was, it was merely chemistry and physics, not engineering. I watched the storm moving away in the darkness as I stood in the parking lot of the Motel 6. There was a fast food restaurant next door, and I was considering it, as I was out of fruit. Sarah, no doubt influenced by her mother, had shamed me into giving up such food. "Slow suicide," she called it.

Earlier that day I had gone to the San Antonio public library. The building was not much larger than the bookmobile that used to drive around my Chicago neighborhood when I was a kid. I got online and read about the dead and missing women of Ciudad Juárez. I had seen it all before, and it was no less shocking or sad for prior knowledge. Next to me, at another terminal, sat an older Hispanic man who, I thought, was reading over my shoulder. He smiled at me.

"Nice library," I said.

"I come here every day," he said.

"Is that right?"

"I wait here while my daughter works."

"I see."

"We live just up in Belen."

"That's far away," I said.

He nodded. "But this is where the job is. We used to live way up near Taos. I had some sheeps." That's how he said it, sheeps. "My daughter thinks I might get sick and she'll be too far away."

"I see."

"It's not like she can do anything. She's no doctor." He paused. "She works at the Lotta Burger. It's a good job. I hope she can keep it."

I thought he was looking at my screen. "Shame about those poor women," I said. I adjusted the monitor to face me more.

"What?" he asked. Then, as if it all came to him at once, "Death comes when it comes. That's what I tell my daughter. I'm ninety-two. I don't want to sit in the library all day. I guess she would rather have me die in the library instead of my own bed."

"I'm sure that's not what she's thinking."

"She's not thinking," he said.

"Death scares people," I said.

"Guilt scares people," he said.

"I'm sure that's not what she's thinking about," I said, obviously without knowing. I looked at his scraggly gray goatee. "Guilt is a terrible thing."

There I was at the dusty edge of the parking lot of that very Lotta Burger where the old man's daughter worked. At least I imagined it was; how many Lotta Burger restaurants could there be in San Antonio, New Mexico? There was only one car parked there, a very out-of-place late-model silver Audi SUV. Beside it, under the yellowish light of the Lotta Burger sign, stood an expensively dressed couple, an older white man and a younger white woman, neither terribly attractive. They ate soft serve ice cream on cones and looked happy. Lightning flashed far off over White Sands Missile Range.

It was hotter in New Mexico.

It was atypically overcast on Thursday morning. The dark clouds had a greenish tinge, and rain was a fairly foregone conclusion. I sat in the front passenger seat of a midseventies Saab convertible, parked at the south end of the Smith's grocery store parking lot. It was Georgia's car. She sat behind the wheel, earbuds in her ears under her gray bun. We were waiting.

I was going to try. Now I was not alone. I had help. I had poets. I did not, apparently, have good sense.

"Do you like music?" Georgia asked me, pulling the bud from her right ear.

"Yes," I said. "Jazz, I guess." It occurred to me as I tried to answer that maybe I wasn't a music lover. I had no real, concrete response to her question. "What are you listening to?"

"You'll laugh," she said.

"I doubt that."

"Jefferson Airplane. Do you know them? Grace Slick?"

"I'm sure I've heard them," I lied.

"'White Rabbit'?"

I smiled stupidly.

"Would you like to hear some?" She offered me her headset and phone.

"No, thanks."

We sat without speaking for a while.

She ate from a bag of Doritos, her headphones again engaged. "This is a great thing you're doing," she said. "Not many people would do it."

"We'll see if I go through with it."

"You will. Can you believe we live in such a world?"

I shook my head.

"Mind if I ask why you're doing it?" She turned off her music, stared with me at the fairly busy parking area.

"I don't know. It's good to help someone."

"Wish more people felt like that. There's so much hate. I used to know Stephen Stills."

"Excuse me?"

"Crosby, Stills, Nash, and Young."

I was lost.

"They were a band in the sixties. Stephen wrote 'Love the One You're With.' You've heard that, I'm sure." She sang a few lines.

"Sounds familiar," I said.

"Things were very, very different back then," Georgia said. "Woodstock. There was a lot of love. Those were the days."

"Yes, they were. The good old days." She didn't detect my irony.

"DeLois thinks you're great. Crazy, but great."

"She's half-right."

Georgia laughed. She looked at the sky. "It's going to rain. Is that good or bad for what you're about to do?"

I said nothing.

"Mexico should be building a wall to protect themselves from us. Don't you think?"

I hadn't thought about politics at all, about Mexicans or Americans, black, brown, or white. I was there to take Rosalita Gonzalez and her friends home. I was there to save somebody, anybody. I needed that.

Across the parking lot, beside the grocery store building, was DeLois's little Datsun. Grace sat beside her; I could see her hair. We had a rough plan that was really no plan at all, it more or less coming down to me sneaking the women out of the market, into the bus, and then driving us to El Paso and across the border into Mexico. I had never been one to take drugs; however, a few well or even poorly prescribed pills would have been very helpful at that moment.

Ernesto was a friend of the grocery store manager, so he and Jaime stood around wearing aprons, pretending to work there. The only thing our plan had going for it was that it was rough. Being rough, it was also elastic. One observation from my last market encounter seemed important and finally comforting: I had seen no guns. Of course, that did not mean that there were no guns, but I had seen none.

An hour passed, the clouds thickening, the air becoming increasingly humid and hot. I was sad about the drizzle because that meant the convertible top had to remain up, and I could have used the air. DeLois and Grace looked to be chatting away, hands moving, heads bobbing. Ernesto and Jaime chain-smoked and leaned on push brooms. Georgia had a book open in her lap, but I suspected she was sleeping. It had been a while since a page had been turned.

I was frightened enough as things stood. I was exercising poor or nonexistent judgment in the face of a superior enemy with far more desire and capability to do harm than I. However, one word turned that fear into outright terror: *poets*.

"My wife is a poet," I said, surprising myself.

"Really?"

"She's published two books."

"What's her name?"

"Margaret Petry."

"I know her work," Georgia said. She was excited. "We read a poem of hers in our workshop."

"Small world."

"It really is, isn't it? Wait until I tell DeLois. Imagine that. I'm going to tell her right now." She unplugged her headphones from her phone and placed the call.

"What's up?" DeLois asked.

"Guess who Zach's wife is?"

There was a long silence on the other end.

"Margaret Petry."

The silence continued.

"Remember? We read her poem in class."

Grace let out a yip. "Oh yes," DeLois said. "That was a good poem."

Georgia looked at her phone. "She hung up."

A couple of minutes later, Georgia offered me a small bottle of water.

"No, thanks."

"So, do you have any children?"

"Bus," I said.

"What?"

"There's the bus."

It was hotter in New Mexico.

There was the bus, looking like a yellow cruise ship docking near the side of the building where DeLois and Grace were parked. There was only one man with them this time. I did not remember him from the compound. Unfortunately, I was easily spotted in this landscape, and even if he saw me from a distance before, I would be remembered. I counted the women as they filed out. Eleven.

"Okay," I said. I slid low into the seat.

Georgia started the Saab. She drove us past the bus and around to the back of the store.

The plan was simple enough, I had told myself, realizing that that alone should have been a very large red flag. But luck had already gone my way. There was only one man guarding them.

Ernesto opened the loading dock door for me. I was immediately shocked by how cold it was inside. I followed him through a wide doorway of hanging strands of plastic, nodded to a couple of men working back there. They seemed surprised to see me, but in no way did they appear alarmed. Ernesto stopped me at a pair of swinging doors with round windows. The man held me back with a hand flat against my chest, his other hand gripping the black rubber cushion of one of the doors. The tightness of his grip told me how terrified he actually was. I was moved by this. This was no mere game, and these people, these poets, knew it. They were simply good people. They were there helping me because they were good and decent people who wanted to do a good and decent thing. On the other hand, I didn't know why I was there.

The plan was simpler now, what with only one guard to be distracted. Grace would take care of that. Grace, Georgia, and the store manager. DeLois would remain in her car, having served many of the Nazis in the diner and so likely to be recognized. Rosalva would walk by all the women in the aisles of the market and whisper to them in Spanish to go to the back corner of the store. Jaime worked on cars and was certain he could get the bus started. He also believed that the key would simply be in it. He claimed no one ever removed a bus key. I didn't question that.

The women began to collect not far from me, near the egg section. Then I saw Rosalita and she saw me. I put my finger to my lips, asked her to remain quiet, calm. There came a woman's scream from the front of the store. The scream startled all of us, perhaps no one as much as me. Then I could hear Grace's voice.

"This man touched me!" Grace shouted. "Manager! Where's the manager!"

"Nobody touched you, lady!" the man barked.

"Molester!"

"Jesus fucking Christ!" the man said.

I moved past Ernesto and waved Rosalita to me. "Rosalita," I whispered. "Vamonos. We've got to move."

"Todos ustedes," Ernesto said. "Vamonos. Ahora."

The eleven women filed through the passage as Ernesto held open the door. The men working in back stopped what they were doing and watched us scurry by. A fat man in an apron held the plastic strands aside for us. Thunder crashed just as we exited the building. The sky had opened up, and a hard rain had arrived. It was mixed with small-sized hail that stung my face slightly when I looked up.

Jaime met us at the corner of the building and led the way to the bus. "The keys were not in it, but I got it running," he told me. "Do not shut off the engine."

We ran by DeLois in her car. She gave me a raised fist.

"Let's go," I said to the women.

They climbed into the bus one at a time, far too slowly for my taste. Each one looked more like my daughter than the last. Rosalita was the last to board. Unlike the others she did not look confused or even scared. She looked determined. She had soft features, but she had hardened them, not into a mask that was her face, but into one that made her face clearer to see.

Jaime took my hand and pumped it vigorously. In his face I could see his admiration. "Good luck, friend," he said. "Remember, do not shut off the engine. I won't be there to start it again."

"Got it. Don't kill the engine." I stepped onto the bus, then turned back to him. "Thank you."

I might as well have been falling in behind the controls of the space shuttle, not that the cockpit of the bus was so foreign—it was, after all, just a big car—but the circumstances were so strange. The bus engine shook the whole structure. I waved to DeLois. I struggled getting the beast into first gear, remembered my father saying "grind me a pound" when I first learned to drive. It was raining very hard, and I could barely see. I searched for the wiper switch, found it almost accidentally. The one giant blade swept across the windshield. I crunched into second and became fearful of the stop sign at the top of the hill. I was certain I would stall if I stopped, so I decided I would keep driving even if there was cross traffic, trusting that any reasonable person would steer away from a big yellow bus being driven by an unreasonable person. I leaned on the horn as I came to the intersection.

In the mirror, I saw the Nazi run screaming out of the grocery store, pulling what I thought was his phone from his pants pocket, but it was a pistol. He fired at us without regard or hesitation but failed, I believed, to hit any part of the bus. Grace, Jaime, and Ernesto ducked back into the store for cover. I became fearful that they were in danger. The hard rain and the laboring bus engine made it so I could not hear the report from his weapon, but I saw the recoil clearly. I wondered where his bullets wound up. As the plan instructed, I turned onto the ramp that led north onto the interstate. At the very next exit I got off, crossed back over the highway, and turned back south. The big old bus roared on the wide road; the poor thing sounded as if it would never stop getting louder, it having only three gears and so no resolve. Unfortunately, noise did not translate into velocity. We were like a fat man running his hardest through sand.

"¿A dónde vamos?" Rosalita asked. She was standing at my shoulder. She, in fact, startled me.

"You should sit down," I said.

She didn't move.

"Siéntese, por favor," I said.

She sat right behind me, leaned forward. "¿A dónde vamos?"

"Mexico," I said.

Rosalita turned to the others. "¡Vamos a Mexico!"

The women cheered. For some reason that prompted me to glance at the gas gauge. I never believed in the optimist/pessimist half-full/half-empty thing, but I saw the tank as half-full, and I knew that we would never make it.

Rosalita came back to me and spoke rapidly in Spanish. I couldn't follow her. "Más lento, please . . . por favor."

"Who are you? What is your name?"

"My name is Zach."

"Zach," she announced to the others.

"Señor Zach," I heard a couple of them say.

"Gracias, señor Zach," Rosalita said.

I nodded. I looked in the mirror and saw nothing suspicious behind us, just semitrucks and minivans, none of which stayed behind us for long. I checked my speed, wondered how accurate the speedometer was, not that the bus could have bettered the speed limit. I paid extra-close attention, afraid that if I did anything unusual—drove too slow or veered into the other lane—a cop would see us and pull us over. I was driving a stolen bus, and for all I really knew, I was guilty of kidnapping these women.

I calculated in my head. It would take them more than an hour to reach the market and the highway from the compound. Perhaps that long to discover that we were not headed north. I had to assume that they would figure that out. I hoped that they did not have comrades, law enforcement or otherwise, that they could call to search.

"Why do you help us?" Rosalita asked, struggling with English.

"Enviaste un mensaje," I said, figuring I owed her the respect of struggling with Spanish. I grabbed the collar of my shirt and turned it up. "Mensaje. You sent a note."

"Sí," she said, understanding. "I send note. ¿Por qué estás haciendo esto?"

I didn't understand her.

"¿Por qué?"

"My daughter told me I had to help you," I said without thinking. "Mi hija me envió. Mi hija."

"I try English," she said.

"Gracias."

She looked back into the bus at the other women. I couldn't see them, even in the mirror.

"Is everyone all right?" I asked.

"Everybody okay."

"Tres horas," I told her. "Mexico in tres horas."

She nodded. "Thank you," she said.

I imagined asking her about how she came to be there, about how she was taken, but I didn't know how to ask and really didn't want to know. The low, dark clouds were scattered across the scape, and so we moved in and out of downpours. The wiper remained on since I didn't know where the switch was. When between storms I could hear just how quiet the women were—no laughing, no crying, no talking. There was the occasional cough.

My phone rang and, like everything that day, startled me. I answered it, finding the big bus wheel hard to manage with one hand. It was DeLois.

"Is everything all right?" she asked.

"Yes. Are you all okay?"

"All well," she said.

"Thank you. Tell everyone I said thank you." I hung up before she could say anything else. I needed both hands for the wheel. Just outside the town of Truth or Consequences the clouds disappeared, and the sun came out. I searched the dashboard and finally found the switch, turned off the wiper. The sun, the hot engine, the situation, made the bus hot. I opened the window beside me. After Truth or Consequences, I pulled off the interstate into a rest area. It was fairly deserted but not empty. There was a family of four at a picnic table. They had an old Labrador retriever that reminded me of Basil. Of the five, only the dog seemed interested in us.

I was careful to leave the motor running. I pulled out my phone to call Lieutenant Deocampo while the women visited the washroom. They moved together, like a quarrel of swallows. I noticed that they all wore the same Adidas sneakers. Jeans, T-shirts of various colors, white sneakers with three red stripes on each side. None of them looked back at me except Rosalita.

Deocampo answered.

"I have them," I said.

His silence betrayed his profound surprise.

"Will you be there?" I asked.

"When?"

I had to step away from the running bus to hear him. "This bus is slow, very slow. Three hours, I think. At least that long to get to the bridge. I don't know how long to cross. There are eleven of them."

Again, the silence.

"Lieutenant?"

"I am here, Mr. Wells."

"Will you be there?"

"I will be there."

Hotter in New Mexico.

Rosalita led them from the small brick building back to the bus. The picnicking family watched them this time. I stood by the open door like a poorly dressed chauffeur as the women, one by one, reboarded, not one looking at my face, each one saying, "Gracias." Without the wind pushing through the windows, the bus had become extremely hot, but the women seemed less bothered or affected by it than I was.

I put the beast into first and pushed forward. Just as I did, a child's ball rolled in front of me and I instinctively braked suddenly. I should not have done that. The bus stalled. We sat there on the asphalt, helpless. The women didn't understand a lot of English, but I believed they caught the gist of my one-syllable, stage-whispered exclamation. To compound the intensity of the situation, sitting stranded in that crippled sauna, the white man of the picnicking family walked toward us. He picked up the ball and came to the door, and I opened it.

"Sorry about that," he said.

"No worries," I said. I looked at the rest of his family.

"Problem with the bus?" He was muscular, short, wore a badly kept blond beard, though his hair was red.

"I guess."

Before I could say anything else, he stepped aboard. He immediately spotted the tangle of wires hanging from beneath the dash.

Rosalita left her seat and moved to stand behind me. Whether she intended the gesture to show that she was not afraid of me or not, that was the effect it had. Somehow the man, as he looked at the faces in the bus, at Rosalita, and at me, was able to ascertain that we were together.

"Church group?" he asked.

I nodded.

He looked over at the highway that was just visible, then down the aisle of the bus out the back window.

"I used to drive a bus," he said. "I was always losing the key. Mind if I help?"

"Please." I started to leave my seat.

"You don't have to get up." He reached past me and grabbed the wires. There was a tattoo on his right forearm, an anchor.

"Were you in the navy?" I asked.

"Marines."

"Same here."

"Semper Fi," he said. "I hated the corps."

"Same here."

"You leave those two twisted together like they are. You take this red one and this green one and just make a spark. Like this." He tapped them together, caused a spark, and the engine turned over. "Rev it," he said.

I did. I kept touching the gas to keep it going.

"Got it?" he asked.

"Thank you."

"Gracias," Rosalita said.

"You bet." He backed out of the bus, looked again at the women. "You folks have a good trip."

"Thanks again," I said.

As we drove away, I didn't know what to think. Had he intuited that these were frightened women and that I was helping them? Was he playing it cool so that he could run and call the police? Whatever, I had to assume that now our direction of travel was known. I got off the interstate at Williamsburg, bought water at a gas station, and decided to proceed south on state route 187.

The roadside was hardly empty, peppered as it was with run-down and shut-down businesses—tire retreads, radiator repair—and the occasional tiny church built out of the same aluminum siding as the shops. There was none of the quaint charm of northern New Mexico down here. There was little traffic, but only two lanes made it congested and slow going. We were another hour into the drive when I noticed that we still had half a tank of gas. The gauge was not working. I didn't know whether there were three quarters of a tank or a mere three quarts; I had no choice but to continue on.

Rosalita somehow detected my concern. "Okay?"

"Everything is okay," I said.

The road turned southwest and ducked under the interstate, continued on the west side of it. The route promised to add hours to the trip, but I felt committed to it. I called Deocampo and left a message telling him we would be later and not to leave if we were not there when he arrived. All had gone smoothly from the first, but now everything seemed to be falling apart.

I stopped at a convenience store with two gas pumps. I got out and walked around the vehicle realizing that I had no idea where the gas cap was. Regardless, I didn't trust myself to be able to re-start the engine even if I did figure it out.

In the little store I grabbed jugs of water and put them on the counter. The cashier looked out the open door at the bus and then gave me a long study. "I got a bathroom around back," she said. She was a gray-haired Hispanic woman. "It's real clean." Though her un-air-conditioned store was as hot as the bus, she didn't appear to mind. "Who you got in that bus?" she asked. I was impressed by her directness.

"Friends," I said. "I'm taking them home to Mexico."

She looked at my eyes, into my eyes.

I looked away.

"Take some bags of chips," she said. "On the house."

I thanked her and left. I looked back as I was stepping into the bus. The little woman was standing in the doorway. She offered a small wave.

Again on the highway, it appeared we were headed into another thunderstorm. The sky grew dark, but at least the temperature dropped a degree or two. Rosalita offered me some water. I drank some and handed the bottle back.

"¿Está bien?" I asked.

She was quiet for a while. "A veces nos llevaron a una ciudad," she said.

I didn't quite understand. Something about going to a city. I nodded anyway. "Pronto."

I became increasingly anxious about being on the little road. It was taking us away from El Paso, and I was afraid I would become hopelessly lost, so I worked my way back to the interstate. This was no better, as I merged the bus into nearly standstill traffic. It was already well past two. I called Deocampo and had to leave another message. His second failure to answer left me suspecting that we were being abandoned.

We inched along. Rosalita's English was about as good as my Spanish. I tried to ask her if everyone was okay and I believe she told me they were hot but all right. People looked up at me from the cars. I felt naked. I was in constant fear of hitting another car. There had to be roadwork or an accident. From experience I knew it could be something as minor as a man changing a tire. Then I saw the flashing blue lights. Of course, I knew it was probably an accident, but I couldn't shake from my mind the possibility that it was a road-block. It didn't matter what kind of roadblock, sobriety, vehicle reg-istration, whatever. I had no registration for the bus and couldn't explain the women. "Yes, I'm driving a stolen bus because I'm tak-ing these kidnapped women back to Mexico." As I said it to myself, I realized that it didn't sound so bad, but it would not have gotten the women back to Mexico promptly, and that had become my sin-gular mission, to see them home. And I had, in fact, stolen a vehicle.

The flashing red light of a fire truck allowed me to breathe. I knew then that it was an accident. It turned out to be a car fire. A leather-jacketed man stood by as firemen sprayed foam on his '64 Mustang convertible. I felt a rush of sadness for the man, surprised I had the energy to feel anything outside my bubble. Once past the scene the traffic flowed. We crossed the state line into Texas.

It was just as hot in Texas.

The bus's engine made a new sound, made it again, then died. I coasted into a shopping mall parking lot. I tried to restart it and was able to get a spark and a turn of the starter motor, but I knew what was wrong. The bus was out of gas. I turned to look at Rosalita, then I stood and observed the frightened faces of the other ten. I waved my arm. "Vamonos," I said.

They followed me out onto the surface of the parking lot. There was a dry cleaner, a defunct computer shop, and a Thai restaurant. From where we stood, I could see the Santa Fe Bridge. We walked. If we weren't conspicuous before, we were now. I looked like some pathetic cult leader. I didn't help matters. I was so eager to get to the border that I walked much faster than I should have, leaving the women to nearly trot to keep up with me. In the heat my khaki shirt was soaked and stuck to me. Finally, Rosalita caught up to me and put her hand on my shoulder. I turned to face her. She was out of breath. I looked at the others, then back to Rosalita. She wasn't not asking me to slow down but with her eyes telling me that everything was okay. I nodded and walked off again, slower this time, Rosalita beside me instead of behind. It occurred to me that I would not be able to express to them that I was not saving them, but that they were saving me. Almost there, we could see that the pedestrian lanes of the bridge were crowded. It was nearly five.

The queue was like the freeway had been. We inched along. I looked back across the bridge, searching for the faces of the Nazis. It was strange. Every white man looked like a Nazi at that moment. Then I recalled the redheaded man who had restarted the bus for me, his blond beard, his anchor tattoo. Thirty minutes later I could see the other side of the checkpoint, but I didn't see Lieutenant Deocampo. I knew the women had no documentation, no identification.

The line moved fast enough. Rosalita stepped to the window first. I stood back. There was a problem. There were eleven problems. Several of the other women talked. People standing in the queue stared at me for some reason. The line had been moving, and now it was not. One of the eleven, the tallest of them, began to cry. Rosalita looked back at me, as if to ask for help. I looked away and into Mexico and saw Deocampo. I put my hand up, shouted for him. He had already seen me, made his way toward us. He talked to the border police. The border police looked at me, at the women. Deocampo waved the women into their country. I watched them go. Many of them were weeping now. Deocampo stared at me, nodded. I threaded my way back through the crowd on the bridge. I remembered having seen a bear.

PERCIVAL EVERETT is Distinguished Professor of English at the University of Southern California and the author of nearly thirty books, including *I Am Not Sidney Poitier*, *Erasure*, and *So Much Blue*.

The text of *Telephone* is set in Dante MT Pro.
Book design by Rachel Holscher.
Composition by Bookmobile Design & Digital Publisher Services, Minneapolis, Minnesota.
Manufactured by Versa Press on acid-free, 30 percent postconsumer wastepaper.